The Marriage
Of
Miss
Jane Austen

A Novel by a Gentleman
Volume I

Collins Hemingway

authorHOUSE®

AuthorHouse™
1663 Liberty Drive
Bloomington, IN 47403
www.authorhouse.com
Phone: 1 (800) 839-8640

Published by AuthorHouse   05/14/2015

ISBN: 978-1-5049-1102-3 (sc)
ISBN: 978-1-5049-1103-0 (hc)
ISBN: 978-1-5049-1104-7 (e)

Library of Congress Control Number: 2015907270

Print information available on the last page.

Cover design by Derek Murphy, based on "La reine Hortense sous une tonnelle à Aix-les-Bains" (1813) by Antoine Jean Duclaux, © *Napoleonmuseum, Thurgau, Switzerland*

This book is printed on acid-free paper.

*To the sweetest flower that ever bloomed
in the garden of John and Priscilla,
Wonderfully Always Herself*

I consider everybody as having a right to
marry *once* in their Lives for Love.

—*Jane Austen*

Part I

August 1802-December 1802

Chapter 1

———

"At one time I believed that a ball was a magical place, where one could find true love and dance happily into the future," Jane said. "But that was when I was seventeen—not six and twenty."

She was about to expound on the point when a crash pulled her attention to the door. She turned to see young Mr. Ashton Dennis barreling into the Upper Rooms like a footman with too much luggage—except that his impedimenta consisted of two silver-coated attendants, a middle-aged couple, and the couple's adolescent daughter. Jane realized that Ashton must have entered at a full run and collided with the attendants, who had attached themselves to him in a futile effort to restrain his momentum, and together the men swept up the unsuspecting family like fish in a net in the congested area where the sedan chairs were being unloaded.

What followed was something like a three-step minuet: The girl, dressed sweetly in pink silk, curtsied to the other ball-goers in her bewilderment and then retreated to the rear; Ashton, straightening his coat, emerged with a smile from the sputtering entanglement of bodies; lastly, in a neat counterpoint, the ball's old and portly master of ceremonies, Mr. Shanking, halted Ashton with an elaborately carved wooden cane thrust forward in a fencing pose.

"I wonder, young sir," said Mr. Shanking, pointing down with his cane first to his own polished black shoes, with their diamond buckles, and then to Ashton's muddy Hessian boots, "why you did not bring in your steed, considering that the beast would be as well shod as the master?"

From all around came the titter of those awaiting the opening of the dance. Ashton was a tall, muscular young man dressed in yellow breeches, dark frock coat, light-colored waistcoat, and those muddy boots. He wore his own hair, whether because of the new fashion or unsuitable political views, it was impossible for Jane to know. Though of imposing size and a confident stance, he reddened and struggled to speak.

Mr. Shanking, looking more French than English in his traditional powdered wig and a florid velvet outfit with gold ruffles, cocked his head and surveyed the room to be sure that the attendees appreciated the skill with which he would now dispatch anyone who dared attend *his* ball unsuitably attired. The two youthful attendants approached to assist Mr. Shanking in escorting Ashton out.

Ashton glanced at his sister and the two Austen sisters as if possibly to call for assistance. Free now to register their astonishment, they snapped their fans open and hid behind them. Their reaction caused him to gather his determination. "M-my s-steed w-would m-make more entertaining company than m-most of the party here," he said. "Have my b-boots cleaned. Now."

"Riding boots are proper attire only for officers in uniform," Mr. Shanking averred.

"If the r-rules apply to the lay-abouts in the M-Militia," Ashton said, indicating the scarlet coats scattered about the room, "they apply to any gentleman."

"If you fail to remove yourself, sir, we shall be obliged to do it for you."

"If you are under the m-misapprehension that you will succeed—when I have sw-sworn my attendance to a lady, my sister—then b-by all means—have a try."

Mr. Shanking's two assistants discreetly stepped back; another, anticipating the outcome, had left and returned with appropriate cloths.

"B-be sharp now," Ashton said, signaling to the new attendant to step forward. "That's a g-good man." When his boots had received a brief but vigorous buffing, enough to restore the remnant of the gloss that had begun the day, Ashton brushed the cane aside, filled Mr. Shanking's surprised hand with a cascade of clinking coin, and strode through him and his young men as through a swinging door.

He approached the ladies, who collectively fanned their faces.

"G-good evening," he said. "S-sister, l-lovely as usual. J-Jane, C-Cassandra." They acted surprised that he had singled them out. "Y-your attendant has arrived," he added. "As p-promised."

Ashton's stutter gave the women a moment to recover their wits.

"What is responsible for the stampede, may I ask?" Jane said.

"Th-the coach broke down," he said. "I had to f-find m-my own way. The horse had no speed, but it c-could maintain a pace."

"Dear Ashton, why did you not stop for a proper change of clothes?" Alethea said. "You know where we are staying."

"I could not leave you alone with all the r-rogues and sc-scoundrels in Bath. It was only twenty miles." He spoke as if the rules of the road precluded fresh clothing for anything less than a full day in the saddle. "I said I would be here in time for the opening."

"Sometimes a composed arrival is to be preferred over a timely one," Jane said.

"I promised," he said.

He loomed over them, suddenly quiet, their dismay making him finally aware that the honoring of his commitment had been negated by his undignified entrance.

"Little brother," Alethea was able at last to say, shaking her head in exasperation.

Despite having always been large for his age, he had earned the descriptor *little* because of his youth—he was a decade younger than Alethea, five years younger than Jane. The brother and sister shared the same black hair color, the same robust complexion, and the same frank expression, but Alethea's build was that of her mother, plump torso and stubby limbs. Barely one and twenty, Ashton combined the most rugged and masculine blood of two families: the long-limbed angularity and fierce energy of his father and the sheer bulk of the men on his mother's side. He towered over not only Alethea but also Cassandra and Jane, themselves tall for their sex; and he was nearly as broad as the conscientiously slim Austen sisters combined. He stood next to the ladies like a stallion beside two greyhounds and a pug.

"Now that you are here, Ashton, what shall we do?" Alethea asked, her expression giving way to a smile of sisterly tolerance that Jane remembered well, from when Ashton was a boy. For years, when the girls were together, he would bang into the middle of the room, jump on the furniture to duel an unseen antagonist, or hurl himself among them and their needlework to demand that they ride with him down to the brook. "It is not our task to entertain you," Alethea would say. Taking him by the ear—for which task even then she had to reach skyward—she would drag him away. Jane, Cassandra, and the other Dennis sisters would pile chairs against the door to ensure their privacy. And they would laugh at his impudence.

"As it's a ball," he said now, "I suggest we dance." His stutter diminished as he became more comfortable. He took his sister's arm. They all made their way through the crowded dome-topped octagon that led to the ballroom. Some were curious about Ashton, but others, offended by the nature of his arrival, resembled the stony figures in the frieze on the wall. The musicians, placed above them in an amphitheater-shaped gallery, had completed their warm-up under the direction of the tie-wigged Mr. Rauzzini. The ballroom, the largest gathering place in Bath, was two stories high. Windows ringed the upper story across from the orchestra. Five large crystal chandeliers lit the floor. The room was painted robin's egg blue, a color that provided pleasing relief to the variety of pastels the women wore. The stringed instruments sent out preparatory strains of the first dance to alert those attendees who had drawn the numbers to open the ball. "J-Jane," Ashton asked. "W-would you care to dance?"

She had not seen him since the death of the Dennises' father eighteen months before. Always tall, Ashton had filled out. He was not the gangling, fumbling youth of before but a powerful young man. As he offered his hand, she was surprised at a new directness in his eyes. Almost immediately, however, she was distracted by his face, which had also changed. He had a high, broad forehead; his cheekbones and jaw were sharp and square. But one noticed the angles and edges rather than the whole. The result was that his face had become stronger yet less defined, as if he had been sculpted from stone that was too hard to be quite shaped into final form.

"Still the troublesome boy?" she asked. "You are the head of your family. You cannot address me as you would a childhood friend, but as a lady in good standing."

"Miss Austen, may I have the pleasure of your company in this dance?" he asked, leaning toward her. He carried the scent of a horse ridden hard, slightly acrid yet not entirely unpleasant to a lady from the country.

"Mr. Dennis, I fear that accepting your invitation would deprive too many young women of an opportunity to dance with you. All of Bath awaits. Surely you do not wish to waste your evening attending to the friends of your older sister?"

"I w-was not m-making the invitation through my s-sister or in regard to her," Ashton said stiffly. "I m-made the invitation to a l-lady with whom I wish to dance."

"Run along, Ashton," Alethea said, putting into words what all three women thought. "We have nothing to discuss that pertains to men."

"Then I rescind my invitation." His movement was that of a conjurer making a coin disappear. "It is invisible. It never happened." Though his tone was sarcastic, his action was a kindness, for if she refused his offer Jane would not be able to accept any other dance invitations later on. Moving away, he gave her a glance that was both inviting and forlorn. She responded with a small gesture of the hand to indicate the single ladies waiting at the other end of the floor.

Though she found him amusing, Jane had no intention of being Ashton's proxy. After his unorthodox entry, he would need someone to establish his credibility with the skeptical socialites of Bath. Jane had ceased to be the belle of the ball, but she was known among the families here; and her air of no-nonsense legitimacy would enable Ashton to move on after the customary pair of dances to the younger women who would be his real quarry. Jane Austen refused to serve as a stepping stone for any man, even a dear friend of the family.

When she had visited Bath as a young woman, the ballroom had been so packed that all one could see were the high feathers of the women's headdresses. (She for one was glad to see the end to this extreme ornamentation. Intended to accentuate a woman's height, ostrich feathers atop a lady's head made a woman look like nothing so much as a large, lumbering *bird*.) Though not as crowded these days, the ballroom still held several hundred people. Many of the attendees were the older, dull, and predictable set: the same women, with the same broad faces and fat necks, white shoes, and pink husbands. There were few couples being *particular*, she saw, and relatively few couples worth watching in case anything began to develop.

Even with the handful of Militia present, a number of ladies lacked partners. War had depleted the ranks of available young men, a fact that should work to Ashton's advantage. She watched him make his way through the clusters of people. By introducing himself to the men, he became known to the mothers or other female chaperones; in most cases he was granted an introduction to their charges.

As with all balls, the young ladies were arrayed according to clique. Ashton was too clever to begin with the wealthiest or prettiest girls; if he found rejection there, he would find rejection from every quarter. He began with the second tier, as it were; not the girls so hopelessly out of their element that his asking would be understood to be a ploy; but the middle group, young women who were socially acceptable but poor enough to accept an offer from any gentleman, regardless of the state of his footwear or his elocution. If she were younger, Jane thought, she would probably succumb to his pluck. She had always preferred to dance than to sit.

She could not find favor with his form and technique, however. When one lacks finesse, one does not necessarily replace it with enthusiasm. Still, he seemed to be enjoying himself, which is more than could be said for herself. An evening of ballroom conversation with Cassandra, Alethea, and passing acquaintances rapidly became tedious. As she circulated, she could not help but notice how all of the attendees, including herself, instinctively positioned their reflections to the greatest advantage in the massive gilt-framed looking glasses on the walls. And they instinctively checked those reflections, as she did now for herself. Yet despite the sharpness of her white muslin gown, the train tied up for dancing; the white, flat-soled satin shoes topped with green shoe-roses; and the green accents of hair ribbon and the frill along her ankles—despite all that she had done to enhance her presentation, she did not receive another invitation to dance.

She was in her own clique, of course, along with Cass, that of women who were stylish if overly stale. Her invitations no longer came from young men on their way up in society but from older men who had stalled or were in decline: unmarried clergy from poorly endowed parishes or lately widowed men of middle age and anxious finance. Even these frayed choices were absent in the thin crowd tonight, this being an off-season event related to tomorrow's hot-air balloon demonstration. Jane and Cass remained on the edge of the crowd, the better to be seen in the hope of a miracle.

"Young Ashton is rather good at making friends," Jane said to Alethea, not a little impressed. They had paused on their circuit, just outside the perimeter of the chandeliers so as to avoid the uncertain mizzle of dripping wax. Ashton had obtained half a dozen partners by sheer force of will, a stuttering determination to make himself known. Though he was like as not to be out of time by half a beat, or to risk damage to his partner's toes while attempting an intricate step, Jane observed that he treated the ladies with a humane good will—even apologizing to the girl in pink, who blushed the color of her dress. He did not at the first opportunity discard one woman for another one slightly higher on the ladder of suitability, as Jane had expected. Rather, his willingness to dance with anyone at all kept him bobbing along somewhere in the middle of the social order. At best, treading the tepid social Bath waters. His clumsy solicitousness toward the women and his determination to give every unpartnered lady her time upon the floor, however, did have an unexpected benefit. Before the evening was out, Mr. Shanking himself—the Arbiter Elegantiarum—began making introductions for him.

"I think Ashton has no other purpose but to enjoy himself," Jane remarked. "It is a rather shocking concept for a ball."

"The best element continues to resist," Alethea said. "There is a limit to what impertinence can achieve."

"He deserves a puff of breeze in his sail," Jane said. On the feint of admiring a dress, she approached the closest group of the well-to-do, a family she had met before. Within a few moments she had the young ladies laughing; soon after, they were found to be shooting admiring glances in Ashton's direction. Jane returned to Cassandra and Alethea with a satisfied smile.

"Observe," she said.

Whispers and fleeting looks spread like fire among dry leaves. Previously, the finest of families had managed to be facing away or busy in conversation when Ashton approached. Now, the same mothers and daughters smiled encouragingly when he turned toward them. The young ladies in particular arranged themselves to be very much in his path as he walked off the floor between sets.

"Whatever did you say?" Alethea asked. "Did you offer them gold?"

"Very much the same thing," Jane said. "To us, Ashton is our noisy and disruptive little brother. But to the single women of Bath, young Mister Dennis is now understood to be the strapping inheritor of the largest estate in Hampshire."

Chapter 2

It was their custom—one might say their obligation—to escort Uncle James Leigh-Perrot for his walk to take the waters at the Pump Room.

When Jane and Cassandra stepped out the front door of their house, every imaginable noise of the city assaulted them. Vendors hawked their wares: muffins, milk, cheese, newspapers. "Hot spice gingerbread, smoking hot!" cried one. "Milk below, maids!" cried another—though the ill-fed city cows produced thin milk. Housewives and servants haggled with the peddlers over the prices of all the food needed for the day's meals, a reminder that living costs were higher in Bath because the Austens could not grow their own food as they had at Steventon. Carriages clattered in and out of the entrance to the Sydney Hotel across the street. Banging and thumping came from the tavern behind them, where workers hauled in barrels of fresh beer and mead. The crowds made Jane long to turn toward the open fields—toward the sun—rather than walk into the heart of the city.

Cassandra enjoyed the elegant newness of Pulteney Street—a clean, broad boulevard lined with classical facades—but Jane preferred rural walks cluttered with sweetbriar and wild strawberries. Raised in the country, she belonged there. The city was where one went from time to time for entertainment and variety, but it lacked the spiritual nourishment necessary for one to set deep roots. Ramshackle old cottages and homes gave the country a lived-in feel, a sense that humanity had been settled there forever; the fields and meadows were as comforting as a child's blanket. In contrast, all of Bath east of the Avon was new, too full of man's noisy accomplishments and too empty of trees and birds. Even Great Pulteney Bridge, which provided a cooling view of the river, saw fit to offend their ears with pounding construction required for repairs from winter floods.

"I have no idea how Aunt Perrot can suffer the city," Jane said after they finally turned right onto Broad Street, putting some of the tumult behind them as they climbed into quieter residential areas containing rows of terraced houses faced with local golden limestone.

"She is a city girl, and we are country girls," Cassandra said, taking Jane's arm. "Each locale has its own rhythms and pleasures."

"God made the country, and man made the town," Jane said. "The rhythms and pleasures of Bath are like to leave me senseless. But—here we are at the Paragons of virtue!"—she referred to the street address, No. 1 Paragon, where their aunt and uncle lived.

Uncle Leigh-Perrot, their mother's brother, stood outside, enjoying the late-morning air. He raised his hat in greeting and smiled. Uncle resembled his sister enough that as children they might have appeared to be twins. One could see at a glance that he had once been handsome, though now his painful gout twisted his gentle face into a grimace. Still, he had an expression in his eye as if he remembered something kindly about everyone he met.

"Cassandra and Jane," he said. "Delighted to see you. How kind of you to wait upon your poor old uncle."

"We were here only yesterday," Jane said. "You sound as if you have not seen us in a fortnight."

Uncle offered his arms to his nieces as if they needed assistance in the slow walk downhill, though it was his gout that made difficulties. "It is the pleasure of seeing such fine young women," he said. "Your father and mother—they do well?"

"Mother expects company for cards and tea," Cassandra said. "Father continues his studies. He will do a short walk in the gardens later today."

"Your father. Always a man of books. Even in retirement."

"He reads now for pleasure," Jane said. "He no longer has to pour over religious works to find a new way to convince an uncertain congregant."

They were more than a block down the street when they heard a peremptory exclamation from behind. They turned to see Aunt Perrot, walking fast. She carried her chin so far forward it seemed to part workmen, maids, and other street plebeians like the prow of a ship parting waves. "Did you not hear me?" she asked. "I have been shouting like a fish-monger's wife. I am quite beside myself." Reaching them, she pulled her Nelson hat down with annoyance. The coquelicot velvet hat had been all the rage since the admiral's victory at the Nile several years earlier. It was the only aspect of Aunt Perrot's wardrobe that was not fresh with the season, because, as she had pointed out before, "patriotism never goes out of style."

"I am ever so sorry, my dear," Uncle Leigh-Perrot said. "We were engaged in conversation. And of course with all the clamor ..."

"You should be more alert," Aunt said. "What if I had been set upon by some highwayman?"

"Dearest Aunt," Cassandra said. "We had no idea you were even coming."

"And highwaymen are rather sparse in this part of Bath," Jane added.

"It is that ridiculous maid's fault," Aunt Perrot said. "I had decided that you should accompany me shopping. I asked her to have you wait until I was prepared. She said she thought I meant upon your return from the Pump Room. Really. We should dismiss her this very afternoon. She misunderstands everything I say."

"I am sure her intentions were the best, dear," Uncle Leigh-Perrot said. "She knew that you do not like to rush your morning ablutions. The important thing is that you have joined us, and you look absolutely lovely."

Aunt Perrot patted her dress as if considering how much better she could have looked with another few minutes of preparation and adjusted her hat as if Nelson might be scheduled for an inspection. "I will let myself reconsider the matter when I have calmed down," she said. "But that girl is on thin ice, I must warn you."

Aunt Perrot's desire to shop took them on a slight detour over to the fabric and millinery shops on Milsom Street, where they browsed for the better part of an hour. Aunt had decided that she needed a new traveling dress for an upcoming journey, though at each shop she announced that London would offer better prospects of finding the right fabric.

"Your trip is *to* London," Cassandra pointed out. "If you wait to shop there, you will have a traveling outfit for only the return."

"It is a difficult decision," Aunt Perrot said. "One never wishes to compromise"—she said this fingering lace that was as fine as any that Jane had ever seen, in London or anywhere else. "Yet one cannot abandon fashion on the coach. It is important that people see who you are. It is the only way to maintain stability and decorum when anyone is allowed to ride inside these days."

"Anyone with a fare," Jane said, though not loud enough for Aunt to hear.

They were directed to a good selection of muslins that had arrived the day before—"from Paris," the shopkeeper asserted, perhaps believing that this was the only city that might upstage England's capital in finery.

"This is very nice material," Jane said, pointing out a white muslin with glossy spots. "Will you have time to have something made?"

"Aunt Perrot," Cassandra said, "Jane and I would be delighted to make you something. We saw several patterns just the other day that would be perfect. We could have it done in a week. That would give us time if you needed any adjustments."

"One does not wear home-made clothes," Aunt Perrot responded.

"There is not a seamstress in town that can set a stitch as perfectly as Cass," Jane said. "And I am very nearly as adept as she. You have been quite satisfied with alterations we have done for you before."

"Alterations are one thing, fabrication is another."

"I do not understand your point," Jane said.

"One dress is made in a shop, and the other is made at home."

Jane and Cassandra exchanged glances. They both understood the difference, but Jane wanted Aunt Perrot to speak it aloud. Either delaying a response for effect or finally responding to the pressure of their eyes, she at last condescended to speak.

"A lady might reply to an inquiry from a friend that she had purchased a bolt of cloth under the duress of circumstances at a shop in *Bath*," Aunt Perrot said, accenting the town's name as if it were a skin condition. "But one could never lay claim to having had a dress made … in the kitchen … by one's … *niece*."

"Thank you for that very handsome explanation," Jane said.

"You, dear," Aunt Perrot replied, "should consider a new evening dress. Yours are looking rather unhappy."

Jane's two evening gowns had graced the ballrooms for the better part of a year. She alternated the dresses so that neither was seen more than once a week, and she disguised them with a variety of accessories. She had even plaited black satin ribbon round the top of one and lowered the bosom, which had such an effect on the gaze of her partners that the alteration had lasted only one ball.

Yet there was no getting around the fact that sharp eyes would identify her dresses as older fashions when the new season began in a month. Frankly, Jane was so tired and ashamed of half her present stock that she blushed at the sight of the wardrobe that contained them. There was also no way of escaping the reality that she could not purchase a new gown until the first of the year, when brother Edward performed his annual kindness of sending Jane and Cassandra five pounds each.

Their perusal of the fabrics had given Jane an idea for her own requirements. While Aunt Perrot settled grudgingly on the material for a dress and pelisse for her journey, Jane discussed with Cassandra the replacement of the lace trim and the practicality of several arrangements of lovely beads that would change her green and white muslin dress from plain to *spotted*. They agreed that the changes would work well—and similar ones for Cass's gown—to revive their modishness pending the receipt of their new clothing money.

Not expecting to shop, Jane and Cassandra had brought only a few pence for tea on their way home. Jane politely asked Aunt Perrot if she could pay back the few shillings Aunt had borrowed on a similar shopping excursion some months back and save Jane a return visit to the shop.

"I am afraid I cannot," Aunt Perrot said, though Jane had seen Aunt deposit into her purse more than enough change to repay the debt. "Your uncle, though, should be able to buy you a ticket for the next ball. That should equalize matters."

"Aunt Perrot, I do not require ball tickets. I require lace and beads. To put a smile on my unhappy dress, remember?"

"I am afraid I cannot help you."

"Might you buy me stockings at Grafton House while you are in London? They would cost about as much as what is owed."

Having no expectation of a positive reply, Jane was not surprised that Aunt Perrot's response was to pretend deafness and stalk from the shop. She rejoined Uncle Leigh-Perrot, who had waited outside where he could engage in conversation with passing gentlemen he knew.

"Off to the waters," announced Aunt Perrot, striding ahead. Uncle Leigh-Perrot needed a boost to put himself into motion. Jane and Cassandra walked with him, ostensibly to assist him if needed but in reality to put distance between them and their aunt. Beginning to flag, Uncle Leigh-Perrot saved his breath for walking. Aunt remained a few paces in front. There was little of the conversation that improved the quality of a walk.

Near the Pump Room, along the colonnade of Bath Street, were additional clothing shops. "Aunt Perrot," Jane called pleasantly, "would you like to stop here anywhere? There's a lovely millinery shop, and we can find some exquisite lace for your new pelisse."

Without looking back at Jane or sideways into one of the establishments, Aunt Perrot raised her hand in an admonishing negative and marched on with almost military determination. The color of her hat made her hair appear in flames. Uncle Leigh-Perrot staggered on his cane, lurching into Cassandra. "Why Uncle," Jane said, "you know how beautiful Aunt looks when we give her clothes a little flair. I was only trying to help."

They came out into the Abbey Church Yard on the north side of the Pump Room, which squared up proudly on its tall grooved pillars and Corinthian capitals.

"We shall leave you here," Aunt Perrot said.

"Uncle's waters—," Cassandra began.

"We can manage the last fifty yards ourselves," Aunt Perrot said. "As you can see, James is somewhat unsteady. I fear that you have worn him out. I find myself fatigued as well. We shall take the chairs home." She pointed to the chair men, a pair for each black-painted leather sedan chair, the white license numbers identifying the rentals. "We will not require you further today. Regards to your parents."

"Good-bye, then, dear Aunt and Uncle," Jane said with all the charm she could muster. "We look forward to tomorrow's walk."

Jane and Cassandra started toward the narrow North Parade Passage. As soon as they were out of earshot, Cassandra spoke. "I cannot believe you asked Aunt Perrot if she wanted to stop on Bath Street," she said. "Were you deliberately trying to antagonize her? You nearly gave our uncle a heart attack."

"She could not repay a debt she owes to me," Jane said, "but she can spend the same amount to ride in comfort in the chairs on the way home."

"Poor Uncle was worn out."

"Someone should antagonize Aunt Perrot from time to time," Jane said. "Why should it not be her namesake? A person with her vanity and her tendency to look down upon others should on occasion be reminded of her own considerable shortcomings." Jane Austen was in fact named for a different predecessor, but Jane Perrot assumed that only *she* could have been the relative being honored; on that basis she assumed responsibility for her niece's understanding of her place in society at all times.

Jane did not slow her pace as they passed Sally Lunn's bakery. She saw Cassandra's wistful evaluation of the goods in the window. "I am sorry, dear sister, but I would spit a bun today," Jane said. "I am so angry."

"It is very well and good for you to display tartness," Cassandra said. "Much is forgiven the younger sister. But our family's future depends on their kindness. Especially considering the state of Father's health."

Jane walked fast, Cassandra lengthening her stride to keep up: to the river; left alongside it; and across the bridge into the new section of town that led to their quarters. Jane was of course as angry with herself for her loss of patience as she was at Aunt Perrot for her determination to treat pettiness as a mark of high character. Jane understood as well as Cassandra the role that these wealthy relatives would need to play in their future. "I should not have lost my temper," Jane said. "I do not mind catering to her moods or her whims. I would provide for them both were they as poor as church mice—if she showed any appreciation whatsoever. But I do tire at her reminders of our dependence. It is not as though we will ever forget. At times, there is a mean-spiritedness toward us that makes me doubt that she has any commitment at all to our side of the family. I sincerely doubt her intention to ever reciprocate our kindness. Certainly not in a way that would inconvenience her."

"Uncle is a kindly man," Cassandra said. "He will see after us when the time comes."

"Uncle Leigh-Perrot does not run that family."

"Well, we cannot spend the next five or twenty years worrying," Cassandra said. "The good Lord will see to our future."

"I would not wager on the outcome of an argument between the good Lord and Aunt Perrot," Jane said. "She would short him a few shillings, too."

"But, really, Sister," Cassandra said, "how could you possibly throw the lace incident in her face?" Having put half a mile between them and the Leigh-Perrots, Cassandra finally allowed herself a smile.

"It was not in her face, it was at the back of her head."

"To this day we do not know whether she stole that card of lace. It is more likely that she was a victim of a swindle. She was acquitted, after all. In any event, you cannot have wished for your elderly aunt to be transported to Australia as a common thief."

"Only because Uncle would have gone with her," Jane said. "No. I do not mean that. But I had hoped to see her chastened by the months she spent in that dreadful jailer's home. It certainly would have made anyone else appreciate what they have. That she was not chastened, that her sense of superiority was indeed reinforced, leads me to believe that she was guilty."

"Jane!"

They had passed Laura Place and were fast approaching Sydney Place.

"Look, Cassy, the balloon!"

Chapter 3

Blooming like a fifty-foot hydrangea in the Sydney Gardens behind the hotel, a hot-air balloon towered over a gathering crowd. "Hurry!" Jane said. The exhibition by a French balloonist was the major end-of-summer social event for Bath. The town had been talking about it all week, and she did not want to miss anything. As a girl, just a few years after the first flights had begun, Jane had seen a hot-air balloon drifting southward over Hampshire. Having chased the balloon for the better part of an hour, she succeeded in getting the aeronaut to wave. This huge blue and gold balloon was the first to come to Bath, an indication of how rare *aerostats* remained.

Jane and Cassandra were, however, rebuffed by the attendant at the entry to the gardens. With the delay and the exasperation of their time with Aunt Perrot, followed by the sudden appearance of the balloon through the trees, both sisters had forgotten that today's demonstration was not included in their season admission. "No change for lace, no change for balloons," Cassandra said. "We really must wake up rich one day."

"Here t-they are a-after all," they heard from behind them. "The l-lovely Austen sisters."

They recognized the man's voice and its stutter. Ashton stood behind them, alongside Alethea. Both were smiling.

"We are so glad that you are able to join us," Alethea said. "We had not heard anything."

"We had planned to attend," Jane said, confused. "But I am afraid that in our haste we left our tickets at home."

"It will take only a minute," Cassandra said. "Our lodgings are just on the other side of the hotel. Please do not wait for us, though. We would hate for you to miss the launch."

Now Ashton and Alethea looked confused.

"But Jane, dear, we have your tickets right here," Alethea said.

"I have no idea what you mean," Jane said. "We have not—"

"D-did you not receive our letter," Ashton broke in, "asking y-you to join us?"

"Ashton bought a book of tickets," Alethea said. "He has been giving them out to friends. We thought to make a small party."

"We have been gone all morning tending to our aunt and uncle," Cassandra said. "We must have missed the messenger."

"How very kind of you to invite us," Jane said, "but we prefer not to be indebted to others."

"M-Miss Austen," Ashton said, "the tickets were only a shilling each to begin with, and they were half price in a book of ten."

"It is not the amount involved but the sense of obligation it creates. Your family already does us so many kindnesses," Jane said. "We will watch from our upstairs window. After the first few minutes, the view will likely be better from there anyway."

"If you do not accept them," Ashton said, "the tickets will go unused. You are too wise a steward of finance to permit such extravagant waste." As always, Ashton's stutter lessened as his confidence increased; and what little stammer remained became unnoticeable as Jane became attuned to his speech. It was the same way when one stepped outside in the evening. At first the crickets were deafening, yet within a few minutes one could barely discern their presence.

Cassandra's nudge compelled Jane to capitulate. They entered on Ashton's tickets, to the amusement of the attendant who had moments before shooed them away. They worked their way through the crowd, which had swollen to several hundred people. Many more watched from outside the gardens, where the view was free. "I fear paid attendance may not meet their expectations," Ashton noted. The balloon was roped off from the audience. At intervals were signs that proclaimed the experience and valor of Monsieur André-Jacques Garnerin, the only man still flying from the first generation of aeronauts. The rest had died in crashes or wisely retired. A small man wearing pants and jacket that repeated the colors and designs of his balloon, Monsieur Garnerin barked orders at half a dozen assistants—locals, Jane guessed, given that Monsieur Garnerin spoke to them through an interpreter and did not seem happy with their work. The balloon was not quite full, nodding slightly as if it still napped before the day's exertions. Every few minutes, Monsieur Garnerin would turn to the crowd with a smile and shrug as if even the most intrepid adventurer faced delays of the most ordinary and infuriating kind.

"The newspaper," Cassandra said, "says that he was the first man to safely parachute from a balloon!"

"That does admit of considerable valor," Jane said, "to hurl oneself into space with nothing but a bed sheet to break the fall."

"I daresay that the parachute may have been safer than the balloon," Ashton remarked. "Look carefully at the skin." The balloon's mottled blue surface was covered with garish gold designs of hieroglyphics and mythological figures and beasts. It was as if the balloon, rather than being the latest advance in science, were itself a creature from a pagan past. The skin was made of silk and paper lined with rubber and alum for fire protection (this, the *Chronicle* had also explained). A complicated netting encased the balloon. The basket for passengers was shaped rather like a chaise longue, an odd but suitably French flourish for a utilitarian vehicle. At irregular intervals across the monstrous surface were another set of smaller gold designs that disguised their nature: patches.

"Unbelievable!" Jane said.

"This pony has been ridden hard," Ashton said.

A flurry of activity drew their attention. A couple of workmen brought wooden ladders to a particular spot on the left side perhaps ten feet up. It became clear in a few moments that they had found a leak. Monsieur Garnerin climbed the ladder to inspect the problem. Using a repair kit, he himself made the first set of stitches to overlay a patch onto the balloon skin.

"They could use a woman's touch," Ashton said to Jane. "How are your sewing skills atop a ladder?"

"Not sufficient to warrant the responsibility."

Monsieur Garnerin gave hurried instructions in French to his assistant, turned over the sewing kit to him, and from the ground oversaw the remaining steps in the repair, in which workers spread what appeared to be a rubber compound over the patch. For half an hour, during which time the crowd became restive, the repair operation carried on. Workmen kept the balloon's brazier stoked to keep the balloon as inflated as possible. The combination of straw, chopped wool, and dried horse manure sent whiffs of smoke through the crowd. The smell reminded Jane of the time when several weeks of severe winter weather prevented her family from the routine process of spreading manure on their fields. The manure pile grew so compressed that it spontaneously combusted, smoldering for days, the heat creating gaps in the snow.

The continuing delay with the balloon caused a few attendees, working-class people for whom the price of admission was a day's wage, to heckle the Frenchman from the corners. Monsieur Garnerin came forward to apologize and seek the crowd's indulgence. His appearance was unusual, for his sloping forehead formed a single line with his prominent nose.

"Sometimes the balloon is damaged in transit," the assistant said, translating for the Frenchman. The assistant had a French accent, but his English was good. "It is a delicate flying instrument, and packing is a complicated process. We should be in the air shortly." He looked at his pocket watch as if uncertain whether "shortly" would be soon enough.

"They had better hurry," Cassandra said. "The wind picks up in the afternoon."

"Meanwhile," the assistant said, "Monsieur Garnerin will be pleased to answer any questions you may have."

Monsieur Garnerin smiled gamely and waited. No one had any queries. The lower orders wanted nothing less than to see the impossible—for a Frenchman to rise into the sky and, with any luck, to return to the earth with a thud. The more genteel seemed awed, as if they lacked the vocabulary to express their skeptical questions. Ashton signaled Monsieur Garnerin to come over. When the Frenchman approached, the two men exchanged bows and introductions.

Alerted by Ashton's notice of the somewhat ragged nature of the balloon, Jane saw similar signs of wear on Monsieur Garnerin. Small, solid, and fit, he had a youthful face and long, dark, wavy locks. Yet the first etchings of age had begun to appear in his face along with a few thin streaks of gray in his hair. Monsieur Garnerin's suit had undergone numerous minor mendings, well done but obvious to a seamstress's eye. It was like an actor's costume: bright and lush from a distance, rather shabby up close.

"You speak French, do you not, Miss Austen?" Ashton asked.

"A little. As do Cassandra and Alethea."

"Would you be so kind as to assist me?" Ashton asked. Not waiting for a reply, he said: "See if he will take passengers."

"Passengers? You cannot be serious, Mr. Dennis."

"I am quite serious. This contrivance is built to hold three or four people. Please, Miss Austen, do as I ask. Is it possible for one to go up in his hot-air balloon?"

Jane had not studied French since she was a schoolgirl. It took her several moments to compose the question, and she was not certain that her phrasing was correct.

Monsieur Garnerin laughed and shook his head—*no!* "C'est très dangereuse. C'est seulement pour le spécialiste."

Ashton did not need help understanding the reply.

"Ask what makes him a *spécialiste*. All he does is set fire to horse dung and climb aboard."

"Mr. Dennis, I will absolutely not ask such an uncouth question of a man who has taken extraordinary risks in the interests of civilization. What is your specialty, after all, except to be rude to people for no reason?"

Ashton regarded her, as Monsieur Garnerin regarded them both. "P-please ask again, w-with the appropriate level of s-subjection, whether he would c-condescend to allow a p-passenger to ride with him for a sum that would indicate the a-appropriate level of r-respect."

Jane doubted whether she could translate into French such a complex request. However, the assistant, who turned out to be Monsieur Garnerin's brother, had been listening. He put the question to Garnerin, leaving out (Jane was sure) everything except that Ashton would pay a great deal of money to accompany the aeronaut. The assistant-brother nodded toward the workmen as if their wages were not entirely secured.

Monsieur Garnerin faced Ashton squarely and said in a thick French accent, "Fifty pounds."

"I w-would not pay five pounds to ride your infernal m-machine, but I would pay one hundred pounds to buy it."

Garnerin's brother translated again, and Ashton asked Jane to confirm the accuracy of the words.

"I am not entirely sure," Jane said, "but I believe the brother considers you dim enough to pay three hundred."

"Anyone with the least acuity," Ashton said to Monsieur Garnerin and his sibling, "can see that you will not have enough francs to return home at the end of your tour. Very likely, this balloon will be left on the dock with most of your other belongings. I offer a fair price to guarantee your safe return home and to make your expedition worthwhile."

Jane was not certain why his comments vexed her so. She reacted at some deep level to an arrogance in which a man with resources felt content to dictate to a man without. "You cannot buy a man's life work simply because you have too much money and not enough sense," she said. "A hundred pounds for an apparatus that will gather dust in your barn? Think about what that amount would do for the poor in your county."

"I am g-giving him the opportunity to c-continue his life's work, not to mention staying out of d-debtor's prison," Ashton said. "I will find a use for this device."

The assistant translated these exchanges as they occurred.

"Two hundred pounds," Monsieur Garnerin said, thickly and nearly unintelligibly.

"One hundred and fifty," Ashton said. "However, if you kill me, my sister will reclaim the fee." Once again Monsieur Garnerin heard the offer via the brother, and had him counter at one hundred and seventy five. He smiled and offered a handshake to seal the deal. Ashton took his hand and said gleefully, "Agreed!"

Jane was stunned at both the speed and the amount of the transaction. One hundred and seventy five pounds was enough to feed her family for a year. How could a man decide so quickly to squander so much capital on a purchase as frivolous as an aging, leaky balloon?

"It is not necessary for you to spend money to prove your worth," she said. "We are more likely to respect a show of restraint."

Ashton waved her off.

By now, the rubber compound had sufficiently cured. Workers increased the fuel in the brazier. The balloon was full and beginning to bounce against its moorings as if eager, after all the delays and negotiations, to be on its way. Perhaps, Jane thought, the balloon felt insulted by the hard negotiations and wanted to prove that its worth exceeded the bargain price. Monsieur Garnerin raised the rope so that Ashton could join him, and Ashton turned to Jane. She tried to think of something to say on his leave-taking, something optimistic but also involving the kindest of regards in case the flight ended badly. In truth she was not sure how to respond: It was beyond belief that someone she knew was about to depart on the most dangerous mode of transport devised by man. To fly!

But Ashton did not wave farewell. He held out his hand to her. "There is room for two. Hurry, now."

For the second time in as many days the women stood transfixed. Alethea said: "Ashton, you have run mad—" Jane shook her head *no*. Upon reaching the basket, Ashton turned back one last time with a beseeching but humorous glance, almost identical to the fleeting look he had given Jane when she refused him at the ball. He made the same coin-disappearing movement as he had the day before, mouthing "Poof!"

"Little brother lacks both mental stability and common sense," Alethea said. "God help him."

Just as he began to clamber into the balloon, he stopped one last time and called out: "Miss Austen, you will be the first woman in Bath to fly!"

The first woman—! This was madness—lunacy. *The first*—. Outrageous. Yet the trees swayed like an expectant crowd. The countryside beyond the buildings, beyond Bath, lay open and inviting. Jane ducked under the barrier, lifted her skirts, and raced to join Ashton where the bright sky beckoned.

Chapter 4

Beyond a modest rocking motion such as one would experience in a small boat setting out from shore, the first few moments aloft held no particular thrall. After the workmen released the ropes and hastened to pull them clear to avoid snagging the balloon, the audience began to murmur with the first flutterings of ascent. There was little sensation of motion. Faces shifted perspective and then began to slide away, as if the crowd were sinking instead of the balloon rising. The interior of the basket was designed so that they could sit as if on an afternoon carriage ride, but Ashton and Jane stood, hands firmly holding on to the chest-high side. Jane risked a wave to Cassandra and Alethea, who observed their departure with identical frozen expressions of disbelief.

Jane was uncertain where to look. Did one continue to watch the varying reactions of the crowd—some joyful, some incredulous, some afraid, a few angry at what had to be a blasphemous violation of God's pure space? Should she look up at the balloon itself, as large as the globe but as insubstantial as Jane's muslin dress? Should she scan the horizon for vistas that were starting to reveal themselves over the buildings? With so much to see from new and ever-changing angles, she did all of these things rapidly and found herself feeling dizzy. She wondered if her face betrayed the same expression of incredulity as Ashton's. He seemed to share her perplexity, her sensation of being overwhelmed, and her excitement. And they had barely cleared the trees!

Streamers set on poles showed that the wind was running to the southeast, but some kind of eddy sent the balloon drifting the opposite way over the Sydney Hotel. She had never imagined how a building would look from above. The central skylight and its smaller companions on either side looked like deep blue pools, giving her a momentary urge to dive in. The colonnaded portico stood out in bright relief in the sun;

the stocky lower level and the tall, thin, elegant upper story formed a congenial pairing. Red-coated valets ran out from under the entryway to see the balloon, which turned north as if to promenade up Sydney Place. A pair of horses approaching from Sutton Street startled at the sight.

The balloon paused as if undecided on its path. They were only a few feet above the roofline. The roofs of this section of row houses had notches and grooves, almost like a key; the pattern was not something one could see from the street. Suddenly Jane saw that they were directly across from her own home. Her parents stood in the window. Along with many other people leaning from windows, the Austens waved at the aerostat. Not a few people waved British flags, though the balloon and aeronaut were French. That the flight was occurring in England was enough to stimulate a show of nationalism.

"Mother, father!" Jane called, returning their gesture with great vigor and leaning so far forward that Ashton felt obliged to clutch at her.

"Mr. and Mrs. Austen," Ashton said in a stiff and strangely formal manner, tipping his hat with his free hand in the requisite manner.

Jane's parents at first responded with great delight at being singled out by the balloonists. But, as recognition dawned as to who was gesticulating and hallooing, their pleasure changed to shock and grief: They grasped instantly that the novelty of their daughter's situation, as exhilarating as it was unforeseen, must be nothing but an astonishing harbinger of death. Mrs. Austen keeled over; Mr. Austen's sudden movement to catch her—deft for a man in his seventies—left his thick white hair in disarray, compounding his expression of fright.

"It will be all right, Miss Austen," Ashton said.

"It had better be, Mr. Dennis."

During these first few minutes of their expedition, Monsieur Garnerin moved from one side of the basket to another, checking clearances, ensuring that the balloon did not graze the hotel or trees, talking quietly to himself with evident satisfaction at their progress.

"Êtes-vous prêt?" he asked. Not waiting for a reply, he dropped a barrage of ballast. The sandbags exploded in the street. Dogs barked and valets and street urchins scattered for cover. Horses tried to run away with carriages. Gentlemen cursed.

"Language most foul!" Jane said, instantly embarrassed that she was focusing on vulgarities as she floated free of the Earth, ascending toward the heavens.

The balloon rose rapidly; the building hid her parents from view. As if seeking its bearings, the balloon swiveled almost completely in a circle. Once free from sheltering buildings and trees, it fell captive to the prevailing wind and surged southeast, sending the carriage rocking in the opposite direction. The balloon and its basket see-sawed over Sydney Gardens like two dancers disputing the lead. Jane caught only a hint of the canal, the bridges, the waterfalls, and the serpentine promenades where she and Cassandra had enjoyed cool walks over the summer. She was certain she caught a glimpse of more than one couple exchanging unsanctioned kisses on isolated benches in the labyrinth. Then they were past the gardens. The balloon continued to rise. Her ears popped. Jane had a moment to take in the buff-colored houses that were almost painfully bright in the sun. The construction on this side of town was all noise and confusion, but from this vantage point she could ascertain the underlying geometric pattern. They were the first to *see* how Bath would look in coming years. The sense of orderly development gave her pleasure. It was a shame that it would take many, many years for the greenery to return fertility to an area sterilized by progress.

Once the balloon stabilized, Monsieur Garnerin turned to his passengers with a cold, professional smile.

"Am I really your first woman?" Jane asked in French, suddenly concerned that her frail form, a wisp compared to Ashton's and Garnerin's, might not withstand the rigors of flight.

Monsieur Garnerin snorted. "Ma première femme? Non."

"Premier *passager* de la femme," Jane said, bristling at the insinuation implicit in his tone.

"Plusieurs femmes vous ont précédé en vol, y compris ma femme. Vous n'avez rien à craindre. Les changements de pression ne vous nuira pas."

"What was that about?" Ashton asked.

"He has taken women aloft before. Including his wife. He assures me that I have nothing to worry about. The altitude will not cause me to explode."

"Mais vous êtes la première *anglaise*," Garnerin said, with a bit more politesse.

"I am the first *English* woman to go up with him," Jane told Ashton, though he seemed to have comprehended the words. He made a palm's up gesture to indicate that he had always known that she was special.

They were high enough now that the woods and farmlands formed a patchwork quilt of light and dark greens, with here and there a stripe of yellow; the texture of the ground from altitude resembled wool and moss. The balloon slowed, reached its apex, and began to drift down. Using a wooden pitchfork, Monsieur Garnerin fed the brazier with more fuel, encouraging a whiff of farm. The basket swayed. Jane's stomach felt momentarily queasy. In a few moments, Monsieur Garnerin had steadied their height above ground. He held up an instrument that measured the altitude. "Interesting," Ashton said. "A variation on the standard barometer."

"We are approximately four thousand three hundred feet," Monsieur Garnerin said in thick but understandable English.

"Is it a good sign that he suddenly speaks our language?" Ashton asked.

"I rather suspect that it portends something disagreeable," Jane replied.

"Monsieur Dennis," Monsieur Garnerin said. "You have purchased the balloon. You have taken away my livelihood." His words were clear despite the French mastication. "With typical English arrogance, you have chosen to embarrass me among my family and your people."

"See here, man, I was rather trying to help you out."

"You were trying to impress this young woman." Monsieur Garnerin bowed to Jane. Reflexively, she returned the courtesy. "You have succeeded. You have what you want, which is everything I have." As he spoke, he unstrapped an odd device from the side of the carriage. It resembled a large umbrella with wooden sticks that went down to a small woven bucket. "But you did not purchase me."

"Monsieur Garnerin," Jane said, "I am sure that Mr. Dennis meant nothing unkind."

"Of course not," Ashton said. "I merely sought to get you back to France before war breaks out again. It is only a matter of time. You could spend years in an English prison. I'm providing you a way home."

"If that were only your intention," Monsieur Garnerin said. "I wish you the very best with your acquisition. Adieu, mes amis. Je vais à la gloire!" With that, he hopped onto the side of the carriage, stepped into the bucket, and pushed off. The balloon heaved sideways, exactly as a small boat would do if someone had rolled off into the sea; simultaneously, it shot up with the release of the man's weight. Below them, they saw the white umbrella structure blossom. Monsieur Garnerin disappeared from view beneath it.

"Il saute en parachute," Jane said, feeling the need to mark Monsieur Garnerin's departure in his native tongue. (Parachute, it occurred to her, was itself a French word: *para*, "in defense of," and *chute*, "falling": to protect from falling.)

After rising rapidly another thousand feet or more, the balloon leveled off. They watched the parachute sway below them, drifting like a dandelion puffball across the green fields.

"This is an unexpected turn of events, but I see no reason to feel distressed," Ashton said. "The weather is perfect. The company is delightful. Monsieur Garnerin will find that an Englishman does not come apart because of a sudden change in circumstance." Ashton's jaw thrust out in determination, but worry lines on his forehead belied his confidence. "We will drift along nicely and settle into some farmer's hayfield. We might exasperate a cow or two, but I doubt that any other damage will be done. A fitting conclusion to a fine adventure."

Jane, however, felt goose bumps rise on her arms. It was not fear, exactly, though she was frightened, but the sensation of increasing cold. They must now be close to a mile high, and the breeze was stronger, pushing them more toward the south as they carried on. She could feel the wind cut through her thin summer dress. The smile she mustered must surely have seemed to Ashton more like a grimace. Yet she could also feel the sun on her face. She relaxed enough to feel the enchantment of the view and understood the lure of the sky: woods and fields undulating beneath them, the blue reflective sheen of streams, a hawk hunting *below* them.

"The wind wants to whisper its secrets," she said.

"What is it saying?" Ashton asked.

"It wants to tell us of faraway countries," Jane said. "Of places we might go, if we had the nerve. France, Spain, Portugal."

"Then it is not so bad?" He had not failed to notice her white-knuckled clutch of the rail.

"I have spent less pleasant afternoons," she conceded.

"I should rather think most of them."

"I am not certain sailing above the woods is superior to walking through them."

"I believe we are starting down," Ashton said, speaking as one might of an approaching appointment.

Indeed, a certain light sensation in her belly was intensifying. For the next minute or so she could tell that the ground was gradually drawing near. Houses and farm buildings grew in size and developed sharper silhouettes. Trees began to clarify their forms.

"It is open land," Ashton said. "We should have no trouble. Perhaps a bump upon landing."

Jane nodded but sensed that something was not quite right. Of a sudden, the ground seemed to be welcoming them with rather too much eagerness.

"We are falling too quickly!" she said. "We went too high. The balloon has cooled!"

Ashton stood motionless. She could see that he agreed with her surmise, but the situation was nothing he could address with either his raw physicality or his pocketbook. She took the large wooden fork and tossed a flake of fuel into the brazier. "Help, Mr. Dennis! I cannot do this alone!"

There being only one pitchfork, Ashton grabbed a flake in each hand and stuffed one and then the other into the brazier. They worked furiously. Ashton managed two or three flakes for every one of Jane's, but for the next thirty or forty seconds their rate of descent increased terrifyingly. Loose straw caught on their clothes as it streamed away into the atmosphere. Rank smoke belched out on them as the new fuel caught fire.

"Keep at it," he shouted. "I think we're catching up."

The horizon was no longer distant but had closed upon them, a sign that they were nearing the ground. At last the sensation of falling eased; the plunge lessened until the balloon came to a halt a few hundred feet above the earth.

"We have done it," she said with some satisfaction. The brazier burned furiously with the huge amount of fuel they had added. Smoke poured into the balloon cavity and swirled out the sides. They coughed through the odor and smoke. At the same instant they both recognized what was going to happen. The balloon began to rise. Soon it was rocketing skyward.

"She is as temperamental as a mare in heat," Ashton said.

"It is like trying to keep the oven at the right temperature for a cake," Jane said. "We must moderate the fluctuations. Feed in a little as we first start to fall. Try not to overcompensate."

They worked out a system by which Jane watched for the first sign of the ebbing of their ascent and Ashton fed the brazier in fist-sized chunks so as not to over-feed the fire. Jane held up one of the sand bags with wry chagrin. They had both been so panicked that neither had thought to use the ballast to ameliorate their fall. Trial and error enabled them at last to steady the balloon and level by level drop it near the earth. The brisk wind, however, thwarted attempts to land. It would have been as dangerous as leaping from a horse at full gallop. As the afternoon wore on, they became adept at skimming trees but covered miles and miles before the wind waned sufficiently to risk setting down.

"Here, do you think?" Ashton said, indicating an expanse of recently hayed land.

Jane nodded her assent. They had to come down sometime, and this appeared their best opportunity. "It is this or a faraway land," she said, for in their bobbing path through the sky they once glimpsed what might have been blue water in the distance—thrilling to consider until she realized it raised the prospect of their being swept far out over the sea.

Timing their fall to just clear a barn, they let the balloon settle on its own in the field. They hoped that the craft would slide a bit and come to a halt. Instead, it bounced with shocking vigor and threatened to sail high enough again to hurt them both in its next dive. Ashton grabbed two lines on the leeward side and hauled with all his might. He succeeded in turning the mouth of the balloon sufficiently askew to dissipate most of the air. The balloon buckled with a mighty exhalation. The basket landed upright with a thud, slid sideways, caught in a furrow, and toppled. Jane felt herself launch; felt herself captured—in the ropes, she thought at first—; felt herself secured like a child in a parent's arms. Ashton took the brunt of the rolling fall onto the ground.

Dirt, dust, hay flew everywhere. They helped each other up. They were dusty, sooty, smelly. Over by the barn came the barking and baying of dogs setting out in their direction while alerting the farm to the advent of airborne strangers. Jane and Ashton hugged in the exhilaration of survival. His left cheek had been raked in the landing. As the farm family drew near—a man coming in a cart, another one on a horse, a handful of children racing their way with the dogs—Ashton and Jane stepped apart. Having returned to earth, they needed to remember its requirements and demeanors. But before everyone arrived, Ashton staked out a position in the sun. With his hands outstretched above him he cried: "Yes! Yes! Yes!" Jane contented herself with smoothing her dress and doing something with her hair— somewhere along the way she had lost her bonnet—but inside she was shouting as exultantly as he.

Chapter 5

Their euphoria did not last long. The farmer jumped clear of the cart and threatened them with his pitchfork—a real one, twice the size of the one from the balloon. His dogs surrounded them, barking ferociously. The children stayed safely behind the cart. The horseman pointed a pistol in their direction. Someone at the house was ringing a bell. They could hear the metallic alarm echo farmhouse by farmhouse through the valley.

"Good of you to track our flight," Ashton said, acknowledging the horseman's strawberry-colored stallion, sweaty from a gallop. "But there is no reason for anxiety. We are a gentleman and lady from Bath on an aerial excursion, nothing more."

"We've been warned to be on the lookout for Buonaparte's spies," the farmer said, keeping them at bay. "The sheriff gave us particular caution about invaders from the sky."

"We are not even at war," Jane said. "How can we be spies?"

"What better time to spy on your enemy than when you are resting up for the next combat?" the horseman replied.

"Come, my good man," Ashton said, "surely even someone from rural Somerset can tell the difference between French spies and a proper English couple."

"You don't look like any English couple I ever seen." The farmer laughed derisively, using his pitchfork to indicate their dusty, straw-covered clothes and smoke-smeared faces.

"A proper English couple would know that they were in the Dorset, not Somerset," the horseman said. In response to their puzzled exchange of glances, he informed them that they were at Fern Down, near the coast. "I assume, as a proper English couple, you know where

Dorset is?" Jane and Ashton could scarcely contain their astonishment: They had covered sixty or more miles in less than three hours.

"It is, I suppose, a coincidence that your balloon flies the *fleur-de-lis* as proudly as a French man-o-war," the horseman said. Indeed, separating the arcane symbols on the surface of the balloon were the iris symbols normally associated with France.

Jane did not find the horseman's looks promising. He was short and swarthy—rather like Buonaparte, she thought. The man sat comfortably astride the stallion, which was tall and lean and despite its lather still pranced as if ready for another gallop through the fields.

"As curious as it may sound," Ashton said, "this vehicle *was* owned by a Frenchman. As recently as this morning. We purchased the craft before parting company under trying circumstances. I assure you that this apparatus is now as English as the Tower of London."

"A curious comparison," the horseman said, "considering you may end up dwelling there."

"The fleur-de-lis was the symbol of French royalty, not of the republic," Jane inserted. "My brother is in the Royal Navy. I assure you he has pulled down a number of tri-colors and set the Union Jack in its place. Furthermore"—she carried on to prevent interruption—"the fleur-de-lis has been part of England's royal standard since James I."

"We are prepared to hang educated spies as easily as uneducated ones," the horseman said. The farmer jabbed toward them with his pitchfork to punctuate the hostile remark. The horseman swiveled his hand to keep the pistol pointed at them as his mount danced. His thin smile was the kind that took pleasure in indignities done to others. The man was almost, but not quite, dressed well enough to justify his disparaging attitude. It was the hat, Jane realized, that gave him away. No gentleman would wear a floppy and sweat-stained hat pulled low over his brow. The man was the overseer, she decided, comfortable with command because of the long absences or laziness of the owner. He treated the stallion as his own under the guise of keeping it exercised.

"Y-you appear to have f-followed us for s-several miles," Ashton ventured. "D-did you not notice that we hailed from the d-direction of B-Bath, and not France?" The emergence of his stutter worried Jane. It was not nerves that brought forth his impediment, she knew; but frustration at the effrontery of the man and his weapon.

"One might d-d-deduce that you had swept in on a south-th-east wind to steal our secrets, and you are now sw-sweeping out on a north-w-w-est wind to carry our secrets back to B-B-Buonaparte."

Jane felt Ashton stiffen. She took his arm, fearful that, regardless of pistol, he might leap at the horseman to thrash him for his mimicry. Fury provided fluidity to Ashton's response. "What secrets would that be," Ashton said, "that Dorset grows cattle and grain? Or that it has the dullest men in all Christendom?"

"Possibly," the horseman said. "Or merely that we are well armed and ready to defend ourselves against intruders."

Jane stepped between Ashton and the overseer. "If you were not so eager to discomfit your betters, you would be more likely to acknowledge us for what we are, English citizens dedicated to God and King," Jane said. She was not one normally to speak of betters or to imply inferiors, but presumption of position was anathema to her. Any rank, whether butcher or baronet, set to the purpose of humiliation was for her among the worst of sins. "Perhaps things would go more smoothly if you were to summon the gentleman you serve."

"I have already done so, lady," the man said. He gave her a mock bow. "He's a captain in the regulars and tends to the Militia hereabouts. We must detain you until he or the sheriff arrives."

His demeanor, however, altered. The reference to his gentleman served as a reminder that there were limits to the indisposition he could impose upon well-to-do if suspicious visitors. He signaled the farmer to call off the dogs, who had not ceased their racket, and rested the pistol on the pommel of his saddle—at the ready, but no longer casting both insult and danger directly at their bodies.

It was only now, as the barking of the dogs abated and the farmer stepped back a few feet, that Jane and Ashton began to appreciate the consternation their arrival had engendered. Their situation was the result of more than an overbearing overseer. Farmers, yeomen, and curious children of all ages had arrived on the run or the gallop. The adults came armed with whatever weapons were at hand: cudgels, swords, the ubiquitous pitchfork, even an ancient pike. Nearly two dozen people now encircled them, and another dozen or so musket-wielding Militia formed a ragged line on the road. Jane recalled that, during the most recent war, rumors of French military balloons caused occasional panics along the coast. Residents became convinced that Buonaparte and his invasion forces would swarm across the skies above the Channel. Since the days of the Vikings, the English coast had always kept a careful eye out whenever the wind blew from the Continent. It was as natural as a farmer watching clouds for signs of storm. For herself, Jane considered worries of an aerial invasion to be … *overblown*. A slow-moving balloon could be swatted from the skies as easily as a fat, lumbering maybug. Compared to a threat from a sea-borne flotilla, Jane could not believe that aerial ships would ever be anything but an annoyance during hostilities. Nonetheless, the fear of death and destruction descending from the heavens had prompted her own brother Henry to step up Oxfordshire's Militia alerts last year, much farther inland than Fern Down.

"We apologize very much for our untimely arrival," Jane said, loud enough for all to hear. "It was not our intention to create a disturbance, especially so close to the coast. We were supposed to take a brief ride in Bath, but our balloonist abandoned us, and we were carried away with the wind."

Taking up her thought, Ashton added: "We appreciate the readiness with which the people of Dorset have responded to possible danger. We apologize for the false alarm. We are not so much the cause of distress as we are *in distress*." He waited a beat before continuing. "Do with me as you will—hang me, if anyone would like to try—but I call upon all decent men to see that the lady is properly tended to."

No one immediately moved, either to attempt a hanging or to assist Jane, until a farmwoman, issuing an annoyed groan as if it were always the women who had to be sensible, stepped from behind the men and took Jane's arm. "Come this way, your ladyship," she said.

"*Miss*," Jane said. "I am only Miss Austen."

The mass of citizen-soldiers parted, and other women came to her assistance as they walked the path to the house. Jane quickly repeated the tale of how they had been blown by the wind a day's hard ride from where they had begun. Commiserating at the danger inherent in their being deposited unexpectedly in a nervous county, and at the state of her dress and hair, they promised her tea and a change into proper clothes. "Not up to your usual standards, perhaps," the farmwife said, "but clean and serviceable considering the circumstances."

"You are more than kind," Jane said. "I feel as if we have ruined the afternoon for the entire parish."

"More excitement than we've seen in a lifetime," she said. "It will give the men something to lie about at the tavern. Who got here first. Who confronted the *strange beast* from the sky." With the phrase "strange beast" she pantomimed a monster from olden days. All the women laughed, including Jane.

Whether because of the sudden release of tension after the harrowing flight and the disturbing confrontation upon landing, or because she recognized the extent of her dishevelment—her finest day dress torn in two places!—or because of the kindness of the women, or because what had just concluded was the most excitement *she herself* had seen in a lifetime, Jane sat at the farm table after the short walk, sipped her tea, and began quietly to cry. This release of emotion set her escorts to clucking at the difficulties that men and their strange compulsion for adventure posed to God-fearing womenfolk everywhere.

Chapter 6

They made quick if bleary miles on the gray road back to Bath through the fields and pastures of Dorset. Ashton drove the chaise, and Jane sat beside him. Behind them rode the overseer, whose task it was to return the vehicle from Bath. It was unclear whether the overseer's assignment was a courtesy from Captain Lovelace, the gentleman of the estate, in providing a high-level escort for their journey home, or something of a reprimand to the overseer for his rough handling of a couple who had become the captain's guests. Because the ride would take most of the day, they had arisen before dawn after a late evening. Two wagons, carrying the balloon canopy and basket, set out with them. The wind had died down overnight so that the ride had begun in a dark chill dew. The wagons soon turned off to the northeast for Hants House. They would arrive at the Dennis home in Hampshire at roughly the same time that Ashton and Jane would arrive in Bath.

"When do you think the messenger would have reached home?" Jane asked.

"Midnight? Possibly later," Ashton said. "He should have got well along before dark. Depends on the freshness of the post horses. I gave him enough money to ensure a prompt turnout, even at night."

"Mother and Father must have been fearfully anxious," Jane said. "Can you imagine? Can you imagine how they felt by evening when they had not heard from us?" When he did not answer, she spoke as if thinking aloud. "What a frightfully stupid, selfish thing I have done."

"That *I* have done," Ashton said. "If I had had any inkling—then, of course—"

One of Jane's first chores had been to write an explanation to her parents about the runaway balloon and to assure them of her safety. Captain Lovelace had seen to its immediate dispatch by his second fastest horse—the overseer's horse being too run out. Jane's note had been as bland as she could construct it given the shortness of time:

Saturday

Dear Father and Mother,

I apologize for the unanticipated sight that greeted you from your window shortly before noon. You had every reason to be puzzled, though I hope your alarm was temporary. Mr. Dennis arranged an aerial tour of Bath and invited me to join him. Cassandra (I assume she is beside you as you read this letter) can attest that the ride was decided on a moment's notice. There was no time to inform you of what we were assured was to be a brief time aloft. We were in the company of Monsieur Garnerin, aeronaut.

However, we had difficulties with our guide, and we were forced to contend with unexpectedly strong winds. Much to our surprise, and because of the remarkable felicity of travel through the air, we were conveyed a great distance to Fern Down in Dorset, close by the sea. We put down gently in a farmer's field, where we were met with great enthusiasm by the residents. The Militia arrived to offer a salute.

Mr. Dennis became fast friends with the local nobility, Captain Lovelace and his wife, who have invited me to stay the night at their home. Mr. Dennis will dine with us before retiring to the local inn. Mr. Dennis and Captain Lovelace labored to ensure that we could begin our return home at first light. It will be a long day's ride (by land!), but we have every expectation of arriving in Bath before dark. Mr. Dennis will send another message ahead if we encounter any difficulties along the way.

Please be assured we are both in good health. Mr. Dennis is of course chagrined at our unforeseen detour and for our delay having created anxiety for you. He has made certain that my accommodations with Captain and Mrs. Lovelace are both comfortable and secure. You will recognize the family name of the Earl of Solent. Captain Lovelace is the youngest son, and a very courteous one.

I trust that this note will put to rest any apprehension that may have occurred as the result of our absence. I look forward to having tea with you tonight in Bath! I hope to tell you about the ins and outs—or should I say the ups and downs?—of ballooning. The serenity of the Heavens is beyond anything I have ever experienced in my life.

Y very affectionate daughter,*
Jane
Fern Down
Dorset

P.S. Please inform Alethea of our situation as soon as possible.
P.P.S. I pray that Mother has recovered.

Jane felt in her own stomach the upset that her family would continue to feel for another eight or ten hours until her safe return. Yesterday's events had been too extraordinary for her to hope that her note had done very much to put them at ease. Jane and Ashton were safe, and Jane had had shelter with a respectable married gentleman and his wife overnight. That knowledge would have to suffice for her parents until she arrived at their door. There was nothing else she could do for now except to hope for the most expeditious journey and for some forbearance on the part of her parents. The farmland through which they traveled, much of it recently hayed, and interspersed with grazing cattle and horses, gave her passing comfort. It was her kind of country. Every mile brought her closer to relief from anxiety. The ascending sun began to warm them, promising of forgiveness.

"At least the weather has been good since the ball," she said. "The road is passable. I never know which is worse, the mud or the dust."

Ashton nodded but said nothing. There had been little in the way of conversation this morning, in contrast to the evening before. After the imbroglio surrounding the landing, their time in Dorset had grown steadily more amusing. Jane remained in the farmhouse until Ashton straightened out matters. The sheriff and Captain Lovelace, a cavalry officer at home on leave, had reached the site of the alleged French landing at approximately the same time. Later, as Ashton oversaw the packing of the balloon and its equipage, Jane was taken to the Lovelace house, where she was able to bathe and wash her hair and dash off the note to her family. Captain Lovelace's wife, Katherine, exchanged the farm dress with something more suitable for dinner. (Jane's original dress was returned, cleaned and mended with compliments from the farmwife. She returned the farmwife's dress with a note of thanks and what little change she had, the customary but in this case insufficient tip.)

Too large for any male clothing in the household, Ashton had had to make do with his suit being dust-beaten by a servant—a young, thin black man, exotic for the area—as Ashton washed himself. Ashton's rumpled appearance at the dining table underlined the singularity of their story. Ashton and Jane regaled the Lovelaces with how they had fought to bring the balloon down safely after the French aeronaut had inconveniently gone over the side. "We did not discover the secret of control until Jane suggested that we act as if we were baking a pie," Ashton explained, demonstrating the care with which they had learned to feed the brazier.

"Captain Lovelace and his wife were so kind," Jane said now. "I must be sure to call on them if I ever find myself in this parish again."

"I invited them to stop over at the House the next time they travel to London," Ashton said. "I hope that I might be able to repay their hospitality promptly. I do not enjoy being in the debt of anyone for very long."

During a stop for refreshment, which the post house advertised as "nuncheon," and a change of horses, Jane stretched her legs with a brief walk around what might generously be termed a village—several dwellings built around a road intersection, much like the Chawton area below her brother Edward's house. As she made her way back, enjoying a late-summer day that had turned marvelously pleasant, Jane saw a barouche, coming from the opposite direction, pull up in front of the post house. As the passengers stepped out, she realized that it was her family—Father, Mother, Cassandra—and Alethea. O dear God, she thought, hurrying to greet them.

Inspecting the underneath of the chaise to ensure that the mechanics remained in good order, Ashton did not see who it was that had freshly arrived from the north. Jane called out, partly to distract her father as he strode toward Ashton, and partly to alert Ashton to his presence. Neither heard her.

"You, sir, are a scoundrel!" Father's voice rang as it might at the crescendo of a sermon on the wages of sin and the fires of hell. "What have you done with my daughter?"

Livid, her father raised his fist to strike Ashton, who stepped back, baffled at first by the identity of his attacker and the reason for such an assault.

"Father! Father!" Jane cried. "I am here. I am all right!" She reached out to him as his fist quivered near Ashton's face like a snake about to strike.

"You!" her father said. "You, girl, will stand aside. For once in your life, you will keep quiet. Silence!" he thundered. "You have taken advantage of your parents' indulgence once too often. You have ... You ..." Jane could see that he was struggling not to say things he would regret; or things that he might not regret but that should never be uttered in public. Jane shrank from him. This was anger her father had never displayed, emotion so strong that it contorted his face.

Arms pulled her backward, dragged her toward the barouche. She was spun about to confront her mother. "What on earth were you thinking?" Mother said, shaking her. "Have you lost your mind? Have you been possessed by Satan?"

Jane's mind whirled. All the Austen children had on occasions felt the sting of a willow branch for childish misbehavior, and the boys had received what Father called a "wholesome thump" the few times it was necessary, but neither of her parents had ever threatened the kind of violence that crackled in their voices now.

"Mother, we were carried away by accident—"

"You left town alone with a man—a man, furthermore, with whom you had no kind of understanding. Have you any idea what a scandal you have created? You not only imperiled yourself with a frivolous desire to ride a hazardous contraption, but you have imperiled our family's standing in town."

"Mother, perhaps we should all calm down," Cassandra suggested.

Mother ignored her. "You spent the night with that ... that ... *man*!"

"I did nothing of the kind! Did you not get our note? We were never alone."

"*Our* note? What *our* is there to speak of? Do you have an understanding of which we are unaware? Have you done things that require an understanding be put into place posthaste?"

"I meant that in order to deliver a message as quickly as possible I sent a single note of explanation for both families."

"Explanation, indeed. How does a proper young lady explain a private ride with a man to whom she is not affianced?"

"We were with a professional balloonist!"

"You were alone with Ashton. In a basket that had all the trappings of a French boudoir! And your dress has been torn!"

"From our landing!" Jane cried. "The balloon collapsed on us."

Behind the chaise, Father continued to rage at Ashton. A tall, thin man with failing strength, Father nonetheless held Ashton's collar with one hand and threatened him with the other. It was all the more frightening that such a weak instrument would square off against a man as physically imposing as Ashton. She could see Ashton's beet-red face between her father's gesticulations, but he made no move to protect himself from a possible blow. At first she thought that her father had actually clawed Ashton, then remembered the injury to his face from the day before. She caught the words "kidnap" and "seduction" from her father.

"We were fighting for our lives!" Jane said, loud enough for her father to hear. "We were trying to discover how to fly the machine after the Frenchman abandoned us. If it were not for Ashton I should have been seriously hurt."

"If it were not for Ashton," her father returned, "you should have your honor intact."

"It was an innocent excursion. We were supposed to rise up a few hundred feet, drift across the Gardens, and set down close to town."

"That is not what Monsieur Garnerin said when he returned to Bath," Mother said. "He told everyone who wanted to hear—and everyone wanted to hear—that Ashton had paid him to abduct you for a private engagement. He all but described a long-planned rendezvous far out in the country."

"Mother, if Jane had planned a secret rendezvous," Cassandra said, "she would not have departed on the most publicized conveyance in Bath history—in full view of half the town."

"But the disgrace!"

"You would accept the slander of a French villain over the word of an English lady?" Jane exclaimed. "Your own daughter? Monsieur Garnerin's actions could have killed us. I cannot believe for one moment that you could believe such infamy about me, or Ash—Mr. Dennis. I cannot believe that you are more concerned over idle gossip than the fact that we could have been killed when that French fraud abandoned us to our fate."

"This is beyond idle gossip. Bath is in an uproar. When your Aunt Perrot heard what had happened, she threatened to renounce us all if we did not banish you."

"So that is what this is about? You are so afraid of that horrid old woman that you would weigh the truth of my actions in the perfidy of her ignorance?"

"All of Bath society has weighed the truth of your actions. *Reprehensible* is the kindest word on the streets today."

Jane was not immediately able to answer. She heard her father again: "So, it was nothing improper you had planned. I am to be thankful that you merely endangered my daughter's life!" The angry comments, snapping through the air like wasps, made both sets of horses jumpy. On the periphery, she saw Mr. Slouch Hat the overseer— Sawyer was his name—smirking at the correction that she and Ashton were receiving.

"It was a foolish thing for me to do," Jane said, "and for that I am abjectly sorry. But I shall not be held accountable for the wicked thoughts and malicious lies of others. I shall especially not suffer the aspersions of a venomous *bi*—." She pulled up at the word she had never said, rarely even thought; yet it was all she could do not to say it now. "—a woman who enjoys nothing so much as rubbing our faces in her wealth. I shall be pleased to march to her home and tell her as much."

Mother stepped back, as stunned by Jane's fury as Jane had been by her Mother's words to her. "Yes, Mother, a common vulgarity describes a woman whose actions toward us are as vulgar as any fishwife's. She believes lies about me involving the most base and degrading behavior, yet I am to hold my tongue out of respect for her? And you join in? You debase my reputation? You imagine the most despicable—"

Unable to continue, Jane collapsed into a half-sitting position against the open door of the barouche. Emotion choked the words in her throat; sobs heaved up from her chest.

"Mother, you go too far," Cassandra said. "Jane confesses her transgressions. They are the sins of an impulsive girl—"

"She is no longer a girl. She is twenty-six years old. Practically a spinster! How will we ever marry her off now?"

"It is not her deeds but your imagination," Cassandra continued, "that has put you and Father into such a dreadful panic." Cassandra gathered Jane in a protective embrace. "She is as sorry as any human can possibly be. Enough. We are done."

Mother stood silent. Her face rippled with fear, anger, sorrow, confusion. She understood finally that while Jane's reputation was damaged, perhaps irreparably, her honor remained inviolable.

"My little girl," Mother said. "Will you never learn to control yourself? Will you never learn anything of moderation?"

Jane nodded, assenting to yesterday's error and to all of the mistakes of her past—things that often encroached upon the borders of society's rules but until now had not sailed so far beyond.

"You shall not return to Bath, do you hear?" Father said. "You, Mr. Dennis, will take your sister and go home. Or to Hades. Anywhere but where my family is. If I see your face in Bath again, I assure you, young sir, you will have your invitation. I do not care about today's conventions, or about my position in society. Set foot in Bath again and I will meet you on the green with pistol at the ready."

Father turned, came around the chaise, shoved Jane, Cassandra, and Mother into the barouche, and ordered the driver back to Bath. As they wheeled about, Jane glimpsed Ashton, immobile as a statue. Alethea stood beside him, arms folded across her chest, her face as cold as marble.

Chapter 7

Jane was remanded to the custody of the parlor for the entire first week after their return to Bath. She did not object. The first and only time she ventured forth on the street, she could feel the heat of opprobrium radiating from the women in the market. The parlor is where she most often wrote, through an unspoken dispensation that left her free after the morning chores. Now, with her mother and sister bustling about as she sat with pen and ink, Jane felt like a child held after school to write "thou shall nots" a hundred times.

Their only visitor in this time was Aunt Perrot, whose arrival encouraged Jane to collect her writings—often a pile of scrap paper—and decamp for her bedroom. Never finding Jane available for a lecture, Aunt Perrot held forth loudly enough over tea on the shortcomings of the young to ensure that she disturbed Jane in absentia.

Letters made up for the lack of social activity. Her father and four of her brothers—James, Edward, Henry in London, and Charles, who had spent the summer with them while on leave from the Navy and was now briefly at Godmersham—were in constant communication. It had previously been arranged for Jane and Cassandra to be taken by Charles to spend the autumn at Steventon. That departure had been delayed so that the sisters could enjoy, along with all of Bath, the marvelous flight of the hot-air balloon. Jane's disgrace now necessitated a more hasty removal from town. Some form of exile was *de rigueur* if one was to expect the tumult to subside. It was a respite by which the socialites could recover their wits, as hens need time after a fox attack before they begin again to lay.

James' Steventon rectory, however, placed them within striking distance of the Dennis family at Hants House. Edward's more commodious manor, though much farther east, lacked the supervision of either a father or a clergyman. From the conversations that Jane could hear among her father, mother, and sister in her father's room, it was evident that the Austens felt torn between the disruption that Jane's presence in Bath caused for the family versus the temptation she might be exposed to in Hampshire or Kent. Her family did not speak directly of Ashton or the Dennises, but rather of "Hants House." It was as if they feared the large brick manor might rip itself from its hilltop foundation and shamble down the valley to entrap their innocent daughter. The matter under argument was whether James' clerical establishment at Steventon or Edward's estate—a home nearly as formidable as Hants House—would provide sufficient protection against such a threat. Or whether in fact Jane and her family should ride out the storm in Bath.

The decision finally made, Jane was summoned before her father at his desk. Mother stood next to him with her hand on his shoulder, almost as if they were posing for a portrait. Despite his health problems, her father showed his usual pink vigor. Mother's lack of teeth caused an inherent stern set to her mouth. Cassandra stood behind and to the left of Jane, either to offer Jane encouragement or to prevent her escape from familial judgment.

"Jane, I believe we have reached a resolution as to where you and Cass will spend the autumn," Father said. His customary selection of books was piled higher than usual on both sides of the desk. Directly in front of him was a stack of correspondence related, she knew, to the matter at hand. The books and letters left a central valley that focused her attention on his face. The nose was the most prominent physical characteristic of the Austens. Her father's was long and thin, an appropriate design for a man who had spent his life preaching the straight and narrow. The severity of bend in her mother's aquiline nose would have rendered her gaze terrifying were it not for the geniality that typically refined her large gray eyes. Their offspring benefited from the blend, with profiles that were prominent without being ostentatious; curved enough to be both individually recognizable and of a family; yet not so arced as to cause distraction. The facial structure framed the directness and intelligence that blazed from the eyes of all her kin.

"It has … been a … *trying* … week," Father said, halting as if to gather more energy. Jane had heard enough, and could surmise enough, to know that her parents were not paralyzed by the ruffled feathers and constant squawking of the self-anointed arbiters of Bath's public perceptions. It was the longer-term harm that might be caused with Aunt Perrot, who had the undoubted power to contravene whatever her husband, their uncle, might provide for them once Father was gone. Jane could prick Aunt Perrot's infinity of pride from time to time with no deleterious effects; but if Aunt ever intended to cut them off from Uncle's inheritance, the balloon fiasco was all the excuse she needed.

"We are, as a family, unaccustomed to being on public display," Father said. "It is unsettling, to say the least, that we must carry on private family business while all the world watches."

"And offers advice," Mother said.

"And gives orders," Cassandra added.

"Therefore this entire matter has become far too hot," Father said. "Let us return to the essentials. We love you, my daughter. The wisest course is to put everything behind us and start afresh. A new beginning, if that were not redundant." He smiled. "We must, however, have a fair understanding of what will happen when you go"—confirmation, apparently, that she was to be permitted to venture within or through the county that housed her family's tormenter. Jane noticed how gaunt Father looked, his skin taut against the bones of his face. A glance at Mother showed that events had worn her down as well. Her skin looked dry and papery; her white hair seemed to have thinned in a week. The cares of the world persuade mortality to step out of the shadows.

"I have not had the opportunity to properly apologize," Jane said. "Not at a time and place where one's parents could be expected to listen. You must know how truly, deeply sorry I am to have put you and Mother in such a position."

"It was this kind of spontaneity that chased away poor Tom Lefroy," Mother burst out.

"It was not Tom but Mrs. Lefroy," Cassandra injected.

"I thought she was my friend," Jane said.

Father raised his hands for silence to avoid another fruitless recapitulation of an ancient and once promising infatuation. After a moment Jane continued. "No one could be more ashamed of the method of conveyance I chose and the alarm it caused."

Her father raised his eyebrows. "Merely the method of your departure? Not the *fact* of your departure?"

"I should never have left without your permission," Jane conceded. "But whatever wrong the impression that my departure created was more than balanced by the wrong done to me by unsubstantiated suppositions of my character. And not merely by the gossips of the world."

"*Jane*," Cassandra said.

"Daughter, when parents fear for their child, they feel equal parts terror at what may have happened to her and anger at what the child did to put herself at risk."

"I am not a child. As Mother constantly reminds me, I live on the edge of spinsterhood."

"One day, dear Jane, you will learn this much: You never stop being a parent. Age does not matter. When your child is in danger, you lose all rationality until you have her safely home in your arms. Which is my way of stating that I was overly harsh, now that we understand the circumstances. I accept your apology for the *manner* of your departure. I have my satisfaction. May we assume you have yours?"

It was unheard of for a father to entreat a daughter. Jane could tell that this ability to understand the force of her feelings came from the force of his own. He sensed that the only way to achieve peace was for both sides to avoid setting off those emotions again. His generosity gave her enormous relief. Her relationship with God was to some degree theoretical. It was only when she was out of her father's graces that she truly understood his sermons on the loss to the soul of heavenly grace. Yet she could not quite hold her tongue. Sensing this, Cass reached for her but was too slow to prevent Jane from speaking. "I am deeply grateful that you and Mother have forgiven me, but another wrong needs to be set aright. However headstrong Mr. Dennis was in commandeering the balloon, however badly he may have treated the Frenchman, there was never a moment when he acted as anything less than a gentleman to me."

"Jane Austen, are you out of your mind?" Mother said.

"Mr. Dennis is a ... *vexatious* ... young man," Jane said. "He is rude, he is arrogant, he is unhindered by the concerns of society. Somehow he brings out the worst in me. That I confess as *my own* shortcoming." She stopped as if uncertain what to say, yet she was not confused. She had created two chambers in her mind. One contained the glories of their flight, of the wind against their faces, of the view of the checkered fields and glistening streams from a mile in the sky, of their fear and excitement, of the freedom and abandon to be fully who they were, of the manner in which they had collaborated to reach safety. The other chamber contained all the rubble from the roof of censure that had collapsed upon her afterward. She paused to ensure that she ordered the contents of the two chambers to keep them separate, so that the repercussions of the flight did not contaminate the moments in the air that she held precious and private. "I will not complain if I never see Mr. Dennis again. But I shall not allow any more calumny to come down upon his head. At least not in this family."

Father held up his hand to halt the remonstrations from Mother and Cassandra. "And I had hoped that my younger daughter would not grow up to be overly submissive," he mused.

Jane had one last thing to say: "Despite his many faults, you could not have hoped to have your daughter in the company of a man more determined to keep her safe, or to respect her person. It is a terrible injustice for you to believe anything less."

"If you say one more thing about that dreadful young man, I shall throw myself in the Avon," Mother said.

"We have two things to weigh, one against the other," Father said. "The first, you must not ignore. What he did was rash and dangerous. We can thank Providence for your safe return. For the second, we must stand corrected. I have made my own inquiries—I am sorry, Jane, but it was necessary. I have corroborated everything you have told us. Mr. Dennis stands redeemed. He is not after all the most despicable villain who ever walked the earth."

Father allowed himself a wan smile. "I can forgive him," he said. "He occupies so much of the form of a man that it is easy to forget that he is barely more than a boy. If this had been a romp with his friends at Oxford, it would have been forgotten in a day. But it was not. The action involved another family's daughter—not something that a mature adult would have ever done. No *man* would have risked a lady's personal safety—or her reputation—for a childish thrill. God help us. Let us hope we are done with balloons."

He waited to see whether Jane had anything more to add. She did not. She lowered her head to acknowledge his conclusion regarding the level of Ashton's maturity.

"You and Cass will go to Steventon as planned. You may have Alethea or her sisters as guests at the rectory, of course, or at Henry's or at Edward's. However, because I cannot trust his judgment, you are forbidden to go to Hants House or to have any association with Mr. Dennis. Are we clear?"

Chapter 8

Jane and Cassandra walked arm in arm, step in step. From behind, only the closest of family or friends could distinguish the two of them, so similar were their forms, dress, and movements. For them both, this was the sweetest season. The harvests were done, all but the gleaning. And good harvests, too: a welcome change from recent years, in which meager grain and the demands of war caused riots over food. Having put up the wheat and hay before the ruination of rains, farmers now dawdled in the cleaning of scythes and leather. Children exhausted the last of a year's pent-up energy in games and gallops, knowing instinctively that the wealth of provisions neatly stacked in barn and bin ensured a full belly throughout the winter. Enough foliage remained in the canopy to daub the trees with a flare of autumnal colors, the careless extravagance of a Master flicking the last of the paint from a brush.

Neither the invigorating isolation of winter nor the green communal excitement of spring nor the languishing headache of summer with its endless social duties had anything to do with autumn. The falling leaves did not signify to them a transition from the longest to shortest days, nor a contraction of the calendar between two harsher times, but a season separate from all others. It was a time of contentment, when nothing needed to be planned or undertaken, when one could enjoy what one has reaped without the need to scramble again tomorrow. It was when nature withdrew into herself, like a harried wife and mother who sends her family away to take for herself a few moments of respite and reflection. When one can do what one wishes to do and not what one is required to do.

Jane and Cassandra walked far out into the fields and cowslip meadows in a wide, meandering loop and came back down the Church Walk past the Digweeds' stone manor and the sycamore-shaded upright brick church in which their father's preachments had recently given way to their brother James'. Jane and Cassandra stopped two or three times to visit over fences and stone walls, to hear what news had accrued in the weeks they had spent with their brother Edward and to inform the neighbors of the elegant affairs at Godmersham. Everyone was pleased to hear of Edward and Elizabeth's rapidly growing family, though Jane and Cassandra exchanged private commentary over what must be their brother's prodigious vigor and Elizabeth's likely yearning for a separate bed.

"It is so good to be home," Jane said. She and Cassandra sat on a small bench outside the whitewashed brick rectory with its red-tiled roof, near the struggling lime tree that James had planted to mark Father's retirement and James' ascension to the church lectern. "I shall never be able to feel the same way about Bath. Our parents must understand our feelings, for they seem determined to keep us constantly on the move."

The two sisters had zigzagged all over southern England since their ostensible move to Bath little more than a year ago. They had had trips to the coast and to Godmersham and Steventon and soon they would go to London to see Henry and Eliza: more than ordinary travel even for the peripatetic Austen sisters. "It does strike one as odd," Cassandra said, "considering that the move to Bath was intended to dramatically increase the number of our potential beaux."

"Perhaps they believe that our continually making an entrance—each time we return to town—will enhance our prospects."

"I do not know whether Bath is tired of us, or just tired," Cassandra said. "I believe our dear parents miscalculated. Neither of us has seen, never mind flirted with, a single suitable candidate."

"Not that there is a surfeit of bachelors in Hampshire," Jane said. "Everyone within striking distance is related. Still, if I am to live and die a spinster, let it be here, of anywhere in the world. In Hampshire, we can at least relax and be ourselves."

Their daily walks in the fields had made Jane understand the depth of her detestation of Bath. It was not because of the unkindness of gossip or the offensiveness of Aunt Perrot. Her roots clung tenaciously here where she had spent all but the last year. She loved to travel, but she also loved to return to the woods of her birth. Her spirit lingered here like a wraith whenever she departed. She felt a palpable ache whenever she knew she was to be away for any length of time, and a palpable joy whenever she caught sight of the elms and strawberries and grass walks that marked their abode.

She was not proud that at least some of her distaste for larger towns had to do with their own stature within society. At Steventon they *were* society. Of the seventy-odd families in the parish, the Austens were among the top five or six, a function of the clergy's prominence in rural parts and of the dearth of wealthy landowners close at hand. If there were a ball or dinner, they were automatically invited; and the hosts were pleased by their acceptance. In Bath they had to maneuver for invitations from the best families and (she was certain) received such invitations only when someone more important had to express regrets. At Steventon, one did not have to look up from a deep well to see the sky. "It is the one great benefit of Aunt Perrot," Jane said, barely aloud. "When she applied herself to our interests, we were able to attend the most extravagant soirees."

Cassandra looked at Jane with a characteristic tilt of her head that normally signaled a confidence about to be shared. Leaning close, Jane was struck by her sister's eyes, the benevolence in them that never seemed to waver. Her face was slightly narrower than Jane's, and wiser. Jane felt that Cass often knew her own thoughts—Jane's—before she herself did. Cassandra's expression shaded from thoughtfulness to entreaty and finally pain. "Shall we never find love?" she asked. "Is it over? Are we never to be happy? Never to embrace the kindness of a man, the blessings of a child?"

"I do not know," Jane said. Usually it was Jane who issued such challenges to fate and circumstance and it was Cassandra who offered assurance that good things would happen in the fullness of time. Jane did not know what to say now, in this reversal of roles. In understanding Jane's thoughts, Cassandra often expressed a preemptive caution that tempered Jane's emotions. Yet it was Cassandra who had expressed in starkest terms the fear that shadowed them on every long, gray, solitary day. Withered beech leaves skittered around them like flocks of wounded ground birds.

"I miss him," Cassandra said. "Still, after all this time. Poor Tom."

Her fiancé, Tom Fowle, had died of yellow fever in San Domingo. All Cassandra had to hold on to was his memory and the legacy of a thousand pounds. It was typical of the consideration that Tom had demonstrated in their every interaction, a reminder that he was thinking of her in any eventuality. Jane knew, though, that Cassandra was troubled every time she received the income from his bequest. The reminder of his generosity was also the reminder of his death.

"His cousin said he would never have taken Tom to the Caribbean as chaplain if he had known of our engagement," Cassandra continued. "We meant only to be discreet, not to make a public proclamation. A mere word, a passing comment … and Tom would be here with me now."

And I would be alone, Jane thought. And immediately regretted the thought.

"And your clergyman!" Cassandra cried.

Jane's clergyman. Neither of them could bear to say his name. They had met at the seaside the summer before last, when the two sisters on a promenade met the two brothers (only one single) also out walking. Jane and the clergyman soon met every day, sometimes both morning and evening. After all the false starts and missed opportunities, after proposals by men she could barely abide, by men who lacked either intelligence or dependability, consideration or sobriety, creativity or hygiene, Jane thought she had finally found a man possessing all the sense and feeling a woman could wish for, in a physical embodiment that might occasion ardor. Cass too considered him very pleasing, one of the most charming men she had ever known—and (Cass was quick to add) very good looking.

When it was time to part that summer, it was agreed that he would join them at the next opportunity, an accord implying that the rendezvous would also bring a proposal. Instead, at the appointed time, they learned—as with Tom before—that Jane's beau had suddenly died.

"I did not have the time to develop the depth of feelings that you had for Tom," Jane said. Cassandra had known him since he was a student boarder at the rectory—here, on these very grounds. No wonder he was uppermost in her mind. Jane rubbed her sister's back as one would do for a sick or troubled child. "Ours was a promising relationship, but whatever expectations I entertained, he and I had hardly moved beyond smiles and repartee."

Cassandra hung her head. "How is it possible that both of us would be so prematurely wrenched from love? From life?"

Cass had faced Tom's death with a degree of resolution and propriety that no common mind could evince, in so trying a situation. An outsider would assume that she had kept her sorrow under control. It was unnerving for her younger sister to see how grave this wound remained. If grief ebbs over time, and if one calculated back five years to its source, one would be overcome with the depth of her suffering then. Cass had not contained her mourning; she had not managed her heartache. She had swallowed her sorrow. The forcible containment for so many years now knotted her with pain. The weathercock groaned, and Jane looked up. The wind tugged it enough to give it voice, the old beaten weathercock that blew down with every major storm. The Austens restored it to prominence on the maypole each time as if it were the national flag that had toppled during battle.

"You lost a man you had loved for some time," Jane said. "I lost a man I was just beginning to love. A good man, but to me, as yet, nothing more."

This was not quite true, and Jane had also not answered the questions raised by Cassandra's lament. Her intent was to offer solace, not philosophy. Like Cass for Tom, she still ached for her loss. She had not had the chance to love him as much as Cass loved Tom, but her loss was more immediate by several years, this loss of a man known only by profession. In avoiding his name, they diminished his reality; they diminished the double catastrophe that had visited them both. Nameless, he had less form and substance than a ghost. Smeared with indefiniteness, his loss was less acute. She would pass over his death obliquely, for to acknowledge it directly would be to put a mirror up to Tom's: The reflections would multiply endlessly until every incident in life would remind them of one of their dead lovers. By reducing the actuality of Jane's loss, they had reduced the actuality of Cassandra's ... and kept them both from going mad.

"I shall weep for the rest of my life," Cassandra said.

Her depth of expression was at odds with the peace of nature that surrounded them. When the pressures of the world subside, Jane thought, the pressures of emotion pour out. She knew that she could never offer solace for her sister's feelings, any more than she would have answers for her sister's questions. It was that time when one spoke in platitudes. Platitudes occupy the space in language where honesty ought to reside except that honesty would crush the soul.

"It is unfathomable," Jane said, "that good fortune will not sometime in the future smile upon us. We shall be happy, Cass. You will see. The world will blush at our happiness. And we shall not apologize one whit."

Chapter 9

Eliza breezed into the room like an actress emerging on stage. Her face was rendered uncommonly beautiful by the intelligent expression of her dark eyes. Those bright eyes appraised her audience, gauging what manner of speech would be most appealing. Her words came with a casual sparkle that could have been achieved only through intense rehearsal.

"What fair maid has danced her ringlets to the whistling wind?" she said. "What fair cousin has come hither on the winds of change?" She greeted Jane and Cassandra with her usual physical affection, hugs and kisses more like those from a young niece than from a cousin many years their senior.

"After the coach from Steventon, I would not be opposed to another flight," Jane replied. The cold rain of their journey had been falling nonstop for a week, making the roads so difficult that the coach had constantly lurched and slewed.

"We might as well have attempted a winter crossing of the Channel," Cassandra said. "I feel as exhausted as the poor beasts who carried us all this way." On half a dozen occasions the passengers had had to get out and walk in sucking mud as the horses struggled to free the coach from axle-deep mire. It had taken an hour of hot tea and a roaring fireplace at Henry and Eliza's house to begin to warm their shivering bones. "It is hard to conceive that politicians brag about the improvements they have made in the roads in the last twenty years!"

"The best I can say of our parents' abode," Jane interjected, "is that it is warmer in Bath without a fire than in London with an excellent one."

"All that matters is that you have safely arrived and begun to thaw," Henry said. "We have a piping hot dinner that should set you down well for the evening. Please." He motioned to the chairs.

The dining room was small but elegantly furnished. Eliza's taste could be seen in the Parisian plate, the expensive silverware, the ornate candleholders, the refined landscape paintings on the wall, the very brightness of the room. As a long-time bachelor, Henry had had the interior decorating skills of an undertaker.

"Tell me all about it. *Votre vol dans l'aérostat*," Eliza said. "It must be delicious if the French were involved." She occupied so much of one's perception that one forgot how small she was—until she asked a leading question with wide-eyed, child-like innocence. Jane was partially convinced that the only reason Eliza had originally married a French cliché—ne'er-do-well young captain with an impressive title and nonexistent income—was to have the excuse of French excess. English scandal had a heavy, leaden weight about it, anchored as it was to national character and expectations; French scandal wafted like strands of mist, fascinating, beautiful, and ultimately inconsequential.

"Let us just say that I was carried away by it all," Jane said.

"I am not sure that we are yet so far *removed* from the *scandal* that we should make light of it," Henry responded. His articulation of the word *scandal* carried no approbation, however; rather, it implied a bemused resignation that his wife would insist upon a tantalizing replay of events. Jane had never believed that Henry, with his taste for the incongruous, had ever personally been offended by what had happened. His concern would have been for all of the emotional perturbation to his parents and to the social and economic repercussions upon them.

"Nothing is worth doing unless it scandalizes someone," Eliza announced. "Especially the busybodies at Bath." She played at scandal as some women did cards. Her birth had had a hint of scandal, she had lived a life that had scandalized some of her cousins—the sterner ones—she still flirted scandalously—"flirtation makes the blood circulate," she claimed—and she carried on in a scandalously independent manner. She once told Jane that she had married Henry because he was the one man who had the good sense not to try to control her—this, while kissing him in a town square in the most scandalous display of affection.

Dinner had the same simple elegance as the décor: lobster, asparagus, and cheesecake. They were most of the way through before Jane completed her recounting of the "matter of the balloon," as it was now termed. She tried hard to play down its dangerous moments, choosing instead to exaggerate its comic elements, but it was not easy, as first Eliza and then Henry interrupted to insist on every twist and turn. Cassandra sat quietly, not offended but perhaps worried that an escalation of the tale might lead to a resurrection of public comment.

Henry told them that he had heard from James that Ashton was already experimenting with the balloon on the farm. He had hopes that it might be used to convey freight, particularly when the roads were in deplorable conditions such as those this week. Jane and Cassandra were of course equally aware of the latest on the balloon, Hants House being but a few miles from the rectory, but by silent agreement the subject was never broached at Steventon.

"It sounds foolhardy to me," Jane said. "The weather that gives us bad roads would wreak havoc on a balloon. I can well assure you that, even in good weather, steering a balloon is like herding kittens. Your cargo bound for Scotland could well end up in Austria."

"Gauging by his record," Henry said, "he will tire of the aerostat soon enough. My teachers at Oxford tell me that Ashton was as bright as any student they ever had, enamored with all the newest discoveries. Yet he had a stubborn refusal to study traditional texts. No more ability to concentrate than a puppy, they said."

After dinner, Jane and Eliza played the piano-forte. Jane made certain that she went first. She played well enough, preferring simpler, more popular music in which she could immerse herself in the emotion without the distraction of complex technique. Eliza was not that much more skilled, but she had the quickness and lightness of touch needed for a classical piece. Going first, Jane enhanced the reception of Eliza's playing; going last, she would have sounded amateurish after Eliza's performance.

When they sat for whist, Eliza mentioned that they had hopes for a trip to France in the spring, "when a lady can cross the Channel without distress."

"It seems an unusual time for a Parisian holiday," Jane said. Henry's venture into banking with two colleagues from the Militia was a relatively recent and quite risky undertaking. She had no doubt that he was prodded into substantive work by Eliza, whose effervescent nature concealed a shrewd mind and a steely determination never to contract a debt. Her current flirtations were aimed at men who could help Henry's career. It did not seem likely that she would jeopardize their livelihood to get a jump on the rest of the smart set with the latest of fashions.

"It is not a holiday," Eliza said. "We hope to claim my estate." When she became pregnant by her first husband, Eliza recognized that her marriage to the dashing and irresponsible Comte de Feullide was beyond mending. She repaired to the security of London to give birth to their child; he repaired to Paris to give attention to his mistress. As a nobleman, he was caught up in *la Terreur* and beheaded, his holdings confiscated on behalf of the people. The only good thing about Buonaparte is that he had restored the rights of property holders.

"Who knows how long the peace will last?" Cassandra asked. "And with Henry's new business ..."

"We are doing well enough," Henry said, his eyes lighting up. "In fact, Eliza and I are doing *marvelously well*. I must inform you of the latest and most amazing intelligence." He paused after this preface, lost in thought. Now in his early thirties, Henry had begun to more closely resemble his father. Though Charles was the youngest son, he had followed Frank into the navy as a teenage boy and developed a seriousness of bearing commensurate with harsh and dangerous life at sea. In contrast, until his marriage to Eliza, Henry had had the air of a sprite about him; he had never taken himself—or, as evidenced by the results, his work—too seriously. His responsibility to Eliza had not in any way turned him dour. On the contrary, it was the depth of his happiness that created the need to provide for a wife and stepson—sweet young Hastings, whom Henry had loved as his own until the boy's death last year. Henry was less of a child himself now; he was growing into his maturity. Yet a difference remained between father and son. Mr. Austen's face radiated kindness, Henry's humor. The two attitudes were related, but the elder man enjoyed the foibles he personally shared with all of humanity, while Henry enjoyed the absurdity that society displayed for his personal enjoyment.

"Tell them the news!" Eliza said, shaking him from his reverie as if to dislodge the information.

"It is such good news that I am still in a bit of a daze."

Jane and Cassandra were not sure what to expect. The confusion and embarrassment caused one's mind to dart to pregnancy. Eliza had taken Hastings' death very hard. She had continued to sparkle in public but told Jane in private that radiating energy outwardly was the only way that she could avoid collapsing into the darkness within. But Eliza—a decade older than Henry—was certainly too old to wish to begin another family. To judge from her figure, she was also not nearly far enough along to entertain a prudent announcement. ...

"It involves the bank," Henry said.

Jane and Cassandra relaxed back into their chairs.

His banking business, he said, had very nearly failed. Its focus was primarily commercial, lending money to farmers and small manufacturers who repaid loans upon the sale of their goods. When hostilities between England and France unexpectedly ceased, military orders—for arms, food, clothing, supplies—were canceled. Small businesses, all owing money, teetered on the verge of bankruptcy. Their collapse would have brought the bank down with them. "Worse," confessed Henry, "I had used tax proceeds for several of the loans." To Jane and Cassandra's horror, he explained: "It is all perfectly legal. We collect taxes long before they are due. The tax collector is entitled to invest the funds in the meantime, to offset collection expenses. I was fortunate enough to receive such funds for my bank."

"Perhaps it would be best to invest next time in short-term bonds," Eliza said drily. "Something safer than a struggling haberdashery."

"What safer bet is there than war?" Henry said. "We have been fighting France longer than any of us have been alive." Fully recognizing the ridiculousness of his plaint, he added: "The Army was our best customer."

"Whatever will you do?" Jane asked. "And what of Edward?" She carried in her head a running calculation of the financial circumstance of each family member, knowing who might be called upon for assistance in hard times. With no way to earn a living, the women, of course, were effectively always in arrears. Father and James were neutral, parsons from a modest district. Frank and Charles were somewhat positive: Their war booty could be substantial, but they went to half-pay whenever they were without a ship. Until his marriage, Henry had been neutral, but Eliza's energy and sharp, supportive mind had moved them to a definite positive. Edward was of course the one superlative, having been adopted by the wealthy Knights. His generosity could be counted on, but he also had invested more than *twenty thousand pounds*, much of the founding capital, with Henry. If that much wealth evaporated through Henry's insolvency, all of the family's reserves would be wiped out, likely forever.

"What needs to be done has already been done," Henry said with some satisfaction and much relief. "We have Mr. Ashton Dennis to thank." The Dennis family had grown rich in trade. The purchase of Hants House by Ashton's father was more than the usual grandiose gambit by a nouveau riche mercantile family to gain respectability. Over time the elder Mr. Dennis had bought land from impoverished nobility who found it easier to play in London than to manage their own estates. Hants House, already the finest holding in Hampshire, had expanded to encompass an estate of more than five thousand acres. The land produced grain, cattle, sheep, horses, and timber, which Ashton's father had used to provide raw materials for his other businesses, many of them engaged in export. "His may be the one truly profitable enterprise in all of agriculture," Henry said. "And his latest and most important customer? ... The Army."

Henry stopped, as if that were the answer to everything.

"Mr. Dennis the younger instantly understood the consequences of the bank's overextension," Eliza said. "Henry was wise enough to go to him immediately to explain the situation." Jane and Cass took this comment to mean that Eliza had sent Henry to Ashton, hat in hand.

"The Dennis family had some funds with us, a token amount to support a local venture," Henry said. "But many of the manufacturers were also suppliers to him. Their demise would have harmed him. And a collapse of the network would have made the Army wary of doing business with any Hampshire enterprises in the future, including Ashton's."

"In conclusion," Eliza interjected, seeing Henry desirous of delving further into the intricacies of the financial situation, "Ashton infused the bank with enough capital to keep everyone afloat through the downturn. It was a curiously generous deed."

"Whatever our short-term difficulties," Henry said, emphasizing his point with a firm push of the spectacles on his nose, "he recognized the solidity of our plans and the value of our long-term prospects. It is as fine an investment as any that could be had in the land."

"That is true," Eliza said, touching her husband again in a way of showing affection as well as support. "But I rather suspect he had other motives." She fixed her gaze upon Jane.

"Ashton has the shrewdness of his father, not to mention his aggressiveness," Jane said. "I agree with Henry as to his rationale. No doubt he was able to extract very favorable terms."

"Very favorable," Henry said, "but not unreasonable, considering the circumstances. Though I must say I never found a more disagreeable negotiator. He rode up to present his terms. We asked for a few days to review them. He told us he was obliged to be home for dinner and would leave in five minutes, with or without a contract, according to our wishes." Henry laughed. "It did not come across as a negotiating ploy. He had made up his mind, and so his victuals were more important than anything we had to say."

"He knows what he wants," Eliza said. "One cannot blame a man for that."

"Whatever his reasons," Henry said, "your impetuous and distinctly obnoxious young neighbor has saved our family."

Chapter 10

28 October 1802

Dear Jane

Surprise, if not outright astonishment, must be the common denominator for interactions between the Dennis and Austen families over the preceding quarter. It was with a mixture of surprise and relief that we greeted the news of the reprieve supplied to Henry's banking concern. It was a revelation that the bank's circumstances had deteriorated so rapidly and to such an alarming degree. According to Henry, he faced certain ruin. It was a complementary shock to learn the identity of the investor who provided the funds necessary for the bank to remain in operation.

The elder Mr. Dennis always displayed more kindness toward our family than the leading landholder might feel obliged to show the local clergy. I always assumed that this was because of the friendship among our daughters. Despite his false steps, the younger Mr. Dennis seems keen to continue good relations. As you accurately and aptly put it in our last family meeting, the manner in which Mr. Dennis carries out his intentions is suspect—or perhaps merely unexpected—and may remain so for some time. Yet recent events confirm the integrity of his intention, an integrity you defended with customary vigor against our parental hesitations.

No doubt, as Henry says, Mr. Dennis's investment is prompted by practical belief in the soundness of the bank's future. Yet there can be no doubt that Mr. Dennis, well understanding the benefit of his actions to several generations of the Austens, acted decisively with particular consideration for our family's interests. Edward pointed out to me that young Dennis could have let all the parties fail, then picked up the bank, some suppliers, and a farm or two for pence on the pound. Do not share this observation with Henry, lest he feel too indebted.

Our young friend found a way that was both meaningful and private by which to carry out a well-deserved penance. This was the action of a gentleman and a Christian, however rough he may be around the edges.

These fresh insights into Mr. Dennis's character require a reconsideration of our family's earlier decision to have the Dennises remain outside the circle of our closest friends. Not only will Henry be obliged to meet with Mr. Dennis regularly, but in this new context only an excess of pride would insist on the exclusion from our company of the family that prevented our precipitous decline.

Further, it was only through James that we realized that our restrictions have had the unintended effect of making you and Cassandra social outcasts in your home county—Hants House being the center of the social whirl where everyone but you and Cassandra gather. I know that you have accepted this taste of limbo with equanimity, but it has been unfair to Cassandra, whose only crime was to escort a sister who at times displays more feeling than restraint.

In summation, you and Cass are free to visit with the Dennis family as you have done in the past, assuming that they also wish to reinstitute the connection.

Our willingness to re-engage with Mr. Dennis and his family in no way absolves you from the responsibility of maintaining your composure as new situations unfold. Mr. Dennis has made two momentous decisions of late involving our family. One was starkly negligent. The other was frankly advantageous. Such inconsistency is the mark of a man who has not yet found himself. This sort of immaturity can lead to other hasty decisions on issues carrying long-term consequences. On matters aerial and otherwise, my admonition is for my beloved younger daughter to at all times keep her feet firmly planted on the ground.

Y^r affectionate father
George Austen
Bath
Somerset

Chapter 11

At the foot of the table sat Ashton, wearing his customary and fashionable light-colored coat, yellow breeches and Hessian boots. Three seats down, across from each other, were Dr. Herschel, the astronomer, and Mr. Collier, the local vicar. This male triad was scattered among seven women of varying ages and dispositions. The unconscious effort to balance the table was defeated by the demonstrativeness of Dr. Herschel, which caused him to take up nearly as much space as Ashton, while Mr. Collier, a small round man with a black bowl of hair, receded into his soup. To the immediate right of Ashton sat Alethea and Cassandra. At the head of the table, by Mrs. Dennis, were Lady Stanley and her daughter Camilla, the latter of whom was being offered for Ashton's consideration along with the wine. Beyond Mr. Collier were Herschel's own sister, Caroline, whose attitude was that of a puppy who fears it has misbehaved, and Jane herself.

"If we were any farther away, we would fall into the orbit of Uranus," Jane remarked, as a way of engaging Miss Herschel, who had assisted her brother for decades with his astronomical studies and had gained a certain repute for herself. Miss Herschel's smile was a crescent moon at best.

Jane saw Miss Herschel examine the large room. Its wood ceiling and wainscoting made it by far the darkest room at Hants House. Three chandeliers, each the size of Jane's own dining room table, responded by seeking to overpower the gloom. Several ornate china cabinets were hidden by the phalanx of servants. Though Ashton's dress was casual, the servants stood by in traditional livery and wigs. Such ceremony was no doubt his mother's doing. No one more fiercely observed tradition than someone new to it.

"At our house, this table would stretch across the kitchen and dining room and out the door," Jane continued. The occupied portion of the table constituted less than half its capacity. "At home, you and I should be eating on the veranda. We would see fewer powdered noses, and more stars."

Miss Herschel responded with more warmth. "I have had many dinners out on the veranda—or at least exposed to the night air. None of the meals were as good as this."

"You have discovered half a dozen comets?"

"Eight, though at least two were also seen by others. It is uncertain as to who had priority."

"And you and your brother are also notable musicians! My parents saw several of your performances in Bath."

"That was many years ago," Miss Herschel said, pleased to have been remembered.

"Come, Miss Austen," Ashton's voice boomed. "T-tell us what has you and Miss Herschel so entertained."

"I was asking how she is able to perfect both her science and her music, with such remarkable results for both."

"It is nothing," Miss Herschel answered. "Patience for the one. Practice for the other."

"Indeed," said Mr. Collier, who seemed annoyed at the lady having been sat next to him. Miss Herschel was so short she looked like a child at the adult table; Jane could see the rest of the company without having to lean around her. Miss Herschel's pasty face was as pinched as a mole's; Jane wondered when she had last seen daylight. Curiously, her brother, who shared the same night hours observing the universe, had the ruddy face of a farmer who has spent his life beaten by the sun.

"You find it remarkable that a lady can excel in natural philosophy?" Ashton asked of Jane.

"I find it remarkable that a lady is so seldom given the *opportunity* to excel," Jane said. "Brother and sister have both accomplished, in two of the most exacting fields imaginable, what would try the greatest genius."

"And you, Miss Stanley, what do you think of the intrepid Herschels, who play concerts by day and find planets by night?"

Camilla's porcelain face was all the more striking for the waterfall of blonde curls that cascaded around it. She had full red lips, a quick smile, and an ample bosom that did not require a cunning network of stays to achieve a great effect. "I should wonder when they sleep," she said.

Everyone laughed, including the Herschels. Camilla scanned the room, both to enjoy the echo of her rejoinder and to enable the admiration of her serene blue eyes.

"Mr. Collier, you have kept your counsel tonight," Ashton said. "What do you think of the latest discoveries of science? Do they help man to better understand his position in the cosmos? Do they clarify his relationship with God?"

As Mr. Collier wiped his lips, considering a reply, Jane caught a wicked gleam in Ashton's eye. At previous dinners the young master of Hants House had sat sullen, made rude toasts, or mocked the various young women being presented for his delectation. One, barely more than a girl, who had eyes that slightly crossed, freckles like a piebald horse, and one of the richest fathers in London, had torn from the room in tears. Ashton had found considerable amusement in the incident until Jane—joined by Alethea—rebuked him afterward. Until this moment, Jane had assumed that Ashton's bonhomie tonight had to do with the proximity of the luminous Miss Stanley.

"One respects much of the work done by natural philosophers in explaining the manner in which God has unfolded his plan," Mr. Collier said. "However, certain philosophers have engaged in such wild speculation that it cannot be reconciled with either common sense or religious belief."

"Such as?" Dr. Herschel asked.

"Is it true that you believe there is life on other planets?" Mr. Collier replied. "Even the sun?"

"If there is life on Earth, why should there not be life on other planets?" Dr. Herschel demanded. "Do you believe God to be stinting in His works? As for the sun, there are large spots that seem to float on its surface. We lack the ocular resolution to determine what they are, but they could be islands or continents capable of sustaining life."

"Rather hot summers, I imagine," Jane said.

"God created man at the pinnacle of Creation," Mr. Collier insisted. "You cannot suppose that man is one of thousands of similar creatures scattered through the stars."

"The Bible says nothing of life on other worlds," Dr. Herschel said. "Besides, species living elsewhere may not be as clever as we. Would that satisfy your Biblical imperative that man must be superior to all?"

"What say you, Miss Austen, Miss Stanley?" Ashton said. "Is it necessary for life to be limited to our planet in order for man to be God's most precious design?"

"If the Mind of God is infinite," Cassandra replied, "I am not certain that any man, religious or scientific, can fathom the infinity of His Creation."

Dr. Herschel: "Well said."

"I am afraid that all of this philosophy is beyond me," Miss Stanley said. "What matters is that we *have* life, and we should enjoy *living*."

Desirous of changing the subject, Mrs. Dennis began to speak, but Mr. Collier spoke over her.

"It is one thing to philosophize about matters on which the Bible remains silent. But do you not, Dr. Herschel, believe that the universe is millions of years in age? What do you call it—*old* time? How can you believe in something that directly contradicts God's word?"

"*Deep* time, Mr. Collier. That is the phrase. Deep space implies deep time. The stars are so far away from us that it has taken millions of years for the light to reach the Earth. And by the reasoning that God himself gave us, the universe must be that old as well."

Jane had always found the starry night breathtaking, filling her with a sense of wonder, but she had never thought of the implications of the heavens being so immense.

"The age of the Earth does not exceed fifty-eight hundred years," Mr. Collier said. "Read the Good Book."

"Fifty-eight hundred *and six*, if you quote Bishop Ussher's calculations from Genesis," Dr. Herschel said, surprising Mr. Collier with his knowledge of the opposing argument. "When dealing with a limited quantity, do not deprive yourself of even a single unit. Most of his calculations come from counting the 'begats' and estimating the number of years in each generation, is that not so?"

"That and the number of years in the reign of each king."

"I have no doubt that the Bishop's work was an honorable effort, representing the best scholarship of his time. Yet explain to me how a man could approximate the number of years for each and every generation—for each and every kingdom—across hundreds of generations—and then provide an answer down to the precise time of day on a particular day and year?"

"His research was exacting."

"Too exact, I fear."

"How so?"

"Honestly, Mr. Collier. After nearly six millennia, can you really believe that a reasonable man could set Creation at exactly six p.m., on October 22, 4004 B.C.?"

"If one arrives at the proper year, understands the Jewish calendar and traditions, knows that God rested on the Sabbath, and counts back six days ... yes. All based on proper authority."

"Yet he used the Bible for only about one-sixth of his calculations. Everything else came from other sources. Could he not have been off by, perhaps, a month, a week, a day?"

"No."

"A quarter of an hour?"

"Not a quarter of a minute."

"Given exactly the same information, you could not calculate the hour of your grandfather's birth, yet you wager all on the creation of the world! Forgive me, but it is precarious in the highest degree to draw chronological inferences from genealogical tables. No, it is not for modern man to apologize for the sloppy time-keeping of his ancestors. Your wine glass is made from sand older than fifty-eight hundred years."

"Rejection of authority is rather in the mode these days. What has it led to? The loss of the American colonies and the French terror! The Bible and the King are God's instruments in carrying out His purpose, for preserving society and protecting us from the ignorant mob. The better sort of society rejects beliefs such as yours that are antithetical to stability and to the teachings of our most sacred Scripture." Mr. Collier glanced about the room to solicit support; probably half the table nodded in agreement. "You verge on heresy that is counter to God, King, and country."

"Well done, sir!" Ashton said. "You have impugned his religion, his patriotism, and his place in society, all in one breath."

"On the contrary, the better sort of society has largely embraced our work," Dr. Herschel said. "Including His Majesty, King George."

"One cannot be sure that he is fully aware of the ramifications," Mr. Collier said. "His advisors—"

"His Majesty requires a full and regular reporting by our observatory. Judging from his *personal* responses, I feel certain he understands our activities—and results—completely."

Mr. Collier looked down, unable to directly counter a favorable report involving the king. "It is a mad enterprise that has the support of a half-mad monarch," he muttered, disguising the comment by speaking into his food. Only Caroline and Jane seemed to hear his remark; Miss Herschel stared at Mr. Collier until, with an oily smile, he turned to engage Miss Stanley.

At this time the army of servants brought in dessert, causing the general conversation to break into separate dialogues. As Ashton was finishing his meal, he asked of Dr. Herschel: "You say that your telescopes lack the resolution to determine the composition of the surface of the sun?"

"Yes. We cannot grind the mirrors perfectly, or keep them from tarnishing."

"What if we could get them closer?"

"Closer ... ?"

"To the sun."

Dr. Herschel pondered the question. "I have considered a mountaintop, but none in England is high enough to be worth the trouble. The Alps are a possibility, but the war, weather, remoteness, cost—"

"I own a hot-air balloon. Flown it more than a mile above the ground. Believe it could go twice that high. Above the clouds, smoke, dust."

"Have you forgotten our difficulties, Mr. Dennis!" Jane did not notice that her expostulation caused a sudden silence. Her head swam with the idea of a heavy, unwieldy telescope destabilizing the balloon. "Have you forgotten our inability to steer? Can you imagine what would have happened if we had capsized with a telescope aboard? Never mind the destruction of a scientific instrument—what kind of harm would it have done to us?"

"Fascinating," Dr. Herschel said. It was not obvious to which part of the remark he was referring. Caroline looked at Jane as if she might be a person of interest. "What is she talking about?" Lady Stanley wanted to know.

"Miss Austen conspired to an aerial elopement with my son," Mrs. Dennis responded. "It was the talk of Bath. I had to insist on his returning to Hampshire at once. I had hoped we had put the disagreeable matter behind us."

"I m-must respectfully c-correct my mother's interpretation of events," Ashton said. "I invited Miss Austen for the balloon ride. She was kind enough to agree. We had some difficulty with navigation, that is all."

"Indeed," Mrs. Dennis said.

Lady Stanley raised her eyebrows.

Miss Stanley smiled as if Ashton's silly diversions were a thing of the past; indeed, her expression contained a grace implying that the misadventure would never have occurred if he had met her soon enough.

Rising abruptly, Ashton offered his hand to his mother. "Stimulating dinner, the best of conversation. I w-wonder now if we might impose upon Dr. Herschel and Miss Herschel to perform for us. Dr. Herschel, I recently had the piano-forte tuned. I hope it meets with your satisfaction." Ashton said all this while drawing his mother to her feet and escorting her toward the conservatory.

"Let us not forget about the aerostat," Dr. Herschel said. "Intriguing possibilities."

"Did you really go up in a balloon?" asked Miss Herschel, latching onto Jane's arm. Her head bobbed below Jane's shoulder. "Do tell ..."

"And afterward," Mrs. Dennis said, her voice wafting from in front, "Miss Austen shall play for us too. She so enjoys those lively Irish jigs."

Chapter 12

Though it was dark, Jane could see through the large windows that a light layer of frost covered the rear lawn. The pond was still; no wind. A layer of low clouds had arrested dawn, and tendrils of fog draped the trees. The new fire behind her had not yet chased the chill from the large room. A few servants moved sluggishly in the background, beginning to set up for breakfast. The start of every day in December required great effort. How had *she* ever struggled out of her mother's womb in such dolorous weather?

After a few scales to warm up her fingers, Jane launched into the "Irish jig" that she had avoided playing the evening before. Miss Caroline, who sensed Mrs. Dennis's desire to embarrass Jane, had continued to play and sing until it was far too late to begin a new entertainment involving anyone else. The song Jane played this morning was actually a ballad, soft and sad in keeping with the gray fragility of morning. She enjoyed the sensuality of the ivory keys on the Broadwood grand piano-forte, which was of much higher quality than she was used to.

"N-Nicely done, Miss Austen."

Jane's startlement caused a missed chord. At any other time of day, Ashton stamped through the house as if measuring the hallways for echoes. At dawn, he came in as silently as the mist. Yawning, he sat heavily next to her on the bench. His thick black hair was in disarray. He had not shaved; his face was as stubbled as a winter cornfield. She turned aside in case either of them suffered from disagreeable breath.

"You really must stop frightening me," she said. "One day I will bang the keyboard so hard it will wake the dead."

"If you hear me approach, you stop playing." His voice was dry and husky, as if he needed a drink of water. He spoke in hushed tones, not because he sought to remain quiet but because he was not sufficiently awake to speak with full authority.

"I play to entertain myself, not a groggy upstart." She signaled one of the servants. Ashton had got into the habit of slipping up on Jane, who rose early to practice in peace; and she had got into the habit of having coffee and buttered toast prepared for him by the servants in the stillroom. The smell of baked bread was beginning to waft its way through the room, giving her hunger pangs. "Where to today, Mr. Dennis?"

Unlike most landed gentry, Ashton kept farmer's hours. His usual routine was to ride the fields with the estate steward before breakfast to evaluate yesterday's work and to outline the projects for today. After breakfast he would inspect nearby holdings, check on one of his manufactories scattered throughout the county, or make a breakneck trip to London or Southampton for meetings with what he called his "mercenaries": lawyers, bankers, shippers.

"Won't know until I meet with Mr. Fletcher. Thinking of clearing another few acres on the west side. Need to do it before the ground freezes or we will have to wait till spring."

They adjourned to a small table when the servant brought their food and drink. Ashton came awake rapidly with a deep draught of coffee. Jane sipped her coffee, an indulgence available only here and at brother Edward's house.

"H-Have you been enjoying your stay, Miss Austen?"

"There is so much entertainment, at times I feel as though I am at the circus," she said. In the weeks of their visit, there had been two balls, several large dinner parties—none quite as contentious as that of the previous evening—a day of shopping and the play *The Way to Keep Him* in Basingstoke. And there were nightly readings or music, through which Ashton had difficulty staying awake. He had struggled even for the Herschels, his most notable guests and by far the most accomplished of the musicians to play. "Cass and I are not wearing out our welcome, I hope."

"By no means. A house this large should always be full of pleasing company." He poured and downed another cup of coffee. "Something I wish to ask."

"Certainly."

"A personal matter. Turned out to be devilishly difficult to obtain a private interview."

"She is a charming creature," Jane said. "I am sure you will do well together. As well as any couple might."

Ashton seemed put aside by her comment, then amused. "You speak of Miss Stanley?"

"You are wise to seek counsel from a friend about an important decision. I am flattered that you would think of me."

"Indeed."

"She is by far the best of the lot, and I suspect your mother grows tired of the parade. You seem taken with her."

"Why do you say that?"

"You have made an art form of sourness with the other candidates. Last night, you were quite animated. You actually asked her opinion of something."

"What do you think of her as a person?"

"Character expresses itself in times of difficulty. I have seen her only here at Hants House, where everyone is happy all the time. Except you, before your coffee."

"Pretty, funny, manners—and the necessary noble family."

"All of that," Jane said. "She has all the credentials one could wish."

"I sense a *however* lurking within your commendation."

"She is the sort of person who professes a love of books without reading, and who is lively without wit. Yet—Mr. Dennis—I am not the person to ask about marriage. I live on the corner of Old and Unattached."

"The best of a bad lot: That is your implication. If she is leading my mother's parade, the parade is going backward. Tell me the truth, Miss Austen."

"I believe she will make you an honest and loyal wife. I believe she will give you the heir you need. I believe she suits you as much as anyone is likely to. And yet ... I believe her feelings for you are more attached to your position in society than to your personality and temper."

"If I ask her to marry me, she will say yes."

"So would every unattached woman of the aristocracy. The question is, what happens after she says yes. After you marry. When she no longer has to flatter you to obtain what she wishes."

"What would you advise a man in my position to do?"

"If your heart is committed to Miss Stanley, then marry her and hope she returns your feelings. If one can give his heart after a single day. Love can as easily blossom after marriage as before. At least that is what people say. If you do not hold her dear, then wait. Find a woman who can truly know your heart. Who wants *you*. With or without your fine estate, your trading companies, your fifteen thousand pounds a year."

"But every woman knows of my wealth and possessions. How will they be able to separate what I have, from who I am? Love me, and not my possessions?"

"You will know her. She will not fawn over you. She will not acquiesce to your opinions to curry favor. She will not submit herself to you for security or gain. She will deal with you frankly, woman to man, and expect you to do the same with her, man to woman. She will expect you to take her or leave her on the basis of respect, honest regard, and genuine affection."

"You speak of the perfect relationship."

"I speak of the only relationship worth having. The only one that can survive life."

"Only two women never fawn over me or curry my favor. Only two never submit to me, deal with me frankly and honestly. One of them is Alethea. D-do y-you understand w-what I am saying, Jane?"

She felt as if she had been suddenly plunged underwater. Her head roared; it seemed that all sound had been extinguished. Yet she could hear the clatter in the kitchen two rooms away, and the comfortable murmuring of staff who had worked there together for years. It was the immediate vicinity that was murky and confused and that made her fear to breathe.

"D-do y-you understand w-what I am saying, Jane?"

"That you find it problematic to marry your sister?"

"Do not mock me, damn you!" Ashton launched out of his chair and halfway to the window in a single explosive movement.

Every polished young woman has a dozen stratagems to deflect the purpose of an unwelcome suitor. One practices firm but gentle rebuffs in front of the mirror almost as often as one practices coquettish ways of saying yes to the proper man. But Ashton? She tried to think of what to say that would maintain the friendship between them, and both of their families, while protecting her independence. She went to him.

"Excuse me, Ashton. You have taken me by surprise. I am at a loss for words."

He gazed across the lawn. Presented in profile, his face carried a stern expression and furrowed brow. His propensity to frown, unless given a reason to smile, was particularly pronounced now. "You must have some awareness of the matter already. I suspect your mother and sister know. Perhaps all the women in the county know. There is a kind of supernatural means of communication among the female of our species. In matters of courtship, anyway. You perceive things before they happen. The way a horse becomes agitated in advance of an earthquake."

"There have not been any earthquakes in Hampshire," Jane said. "At least, not in my memory." This was all she could think to say, so thrown was she by his analogy.

"But you now comprehend the purpose of the interview," he said. "Is it possible, Miss Austen, to give some indication of your leaning—before, perhaps, I broach a subject that might discomfit us both?"

"Your implication has discomfited me already! How am I to reply to a question that has not been asked? A question that may not even *be* asked? Suppose you intend to seek my thoughts on … on … the possibility of a new coach service into London. We should have a perfectly nonsensical conversation."

"The imperative question between a man and woman does not involve coach service." He strode to and fro, with a pause at each turn during which he again fixed his gaze across the lawn as if in search of something. The sky had brightened, though the frost remained. She had the strangest idea: Perhaps Ashton had, in advance, written out phrases on the frost to guide his proposal.

Kindly words of rejection fell completely out of her head. It was as though she had prepared a cake and then dropped it at her feet. She was empty handed; empty tongued. He turned to her, arms folded. Despite his effort to maintain a neutral expression, as if a positive or negative reaction would content him equally well, the face has a way of signaling the answer it genuinely hopes to have. Even in normal moments of stillness he had a manner of looking ready to spring. His stance now implied that a negative reply would send him crashing through the windows.

"Y-you must k-know my feelings, Jane. And I have reason to believe you return them."

"I assure you, sir, I know nothing of your feelings. Not these."

"I have loved you since I was a boy—since I understood that girls were different from boys—since I realized that you were different from other girls."

"Childish absurdity."

"I used to burst in on you and my sisters to be in your company."

"Boyhood exuberance."

"I followed you around at dances!"

"Youthful impertinence."

"You rode with me in a balloon!"

"Why does everyone speak of that aerostat as if it were a bawdy house!"

"We shared an adventure. With me, you forget society."

"I confess the attraction of adventure. I confess the enjoyment of your company. Neither is a crime, nor a commitment."

She could not help but feel regard for him. His decency and generosity were beyond reproach. And the considerations of her mother and sister—and her own security, of course—made his interest abundantly attractive in every objective sense. Who would not be tempted at the idea of resolving all of life's cares with a single word? She could not resist a guilty pleasure at the plaintiveness in his eyes.

"Ashton, there you are!" Looking as if she had dressed hurriedly and put up her own hair, his mother entered the room. "And Miss Austen, of course. I thought I heard the piano being abused." Mrs. Dennis glanced at the table set with the food and service. "A tête-à-tête, I see. Well, well."

Chapter 13

As Mrs. Dennis soon made it apparent that she would remain indefinitely, Ashton took his leave. The estate steward, Mr. Fletcher, was likely already waiting for him. "Miss Austen, pleasant chat. Perhaps we can continue this afternoon." He nodded good-bye to his mother.

"Please join me," Mrs. Dennis said, indicating the table where Ashton and Jane had been sitting. A servant cleared away the dishes and brought fresh ones. Mrs. Dennis told the girl to also take away the "disgusting brew" and bring her a dish of tea.

"Miss Austen, for as long as I have known you, you have been a person of plain speech."

"Yes, ma'am."

"So I am going to speak to you plainly: Stay away from my son."

"Madam?"

"You have been coming to our balls for a decade. During that time you have thrown yourself at every eligible young man with no regard for modesty or decorum."

"If accepting an invitation to dance is immodest, I am a wanton woman."

"You will not dig your insolent claws into Ashton. He has better things in store."

"Like the women you bring to him once or twice a week—the ones who will trade *their* bodies for *his* wealth?"

"Those women are from the finest families in the kingdom."

"From families that sell their daughters for material gain, do you mean? To people who will buy them in exchange for a title. Any day now, England will outlaw the slave trade. What shall you do then?"

"Do not bandy words with me, young lady. You have been arranging assignations with Ashton—walks, early breakfasts, secret meetings under my very nose!"

"Mr. Dennis has shown me the courtesy of seeking out my company from time to time. I have neither encouraged nor rebuffed him. We are friends."

"I interrupted a rendezvous not five minutes ago! Quite a coze in front of the fire! Do you think I am blind?"

"On the contrary, I think you see everything that goes on at Hants House. And a great deal that does not."

"Do not test me. I will send you packing before Ashton returns."

"Exactly the stratagem a clever girl would employ to guarantee his galloping after."

Mrs. Dennis examined Jane with unblinking pitiless eyes. Whatever the outcome of this encounter, or of Ashton's unexpected intentions earlier, Jane saw no reason to court the enmity of this formidable woman. "Mrs. Dennis, I feel that I have stumbled into an argument. Ashton—Mr. Dennis—came down early this morning to seek my opinion of Miss Stanley. He too appreciates my plain speech. I told him that she had all the qualities most men sought in a wife and that, if he cared for her, he should marry her."

Jane's confident response, and her apparent support of the latest candidate, took Mrs. Dennis aback. She sipped her tea, found it lacking, and ordered fresh tea-things. For all the years that the families had known each other, Jane had had very little personal dealing with the matriarch. Mrs. Dennis had left the child-rearing to a succession of nurses and governesses. She appeared at meals to correct and occasionally scold her girls; she inspected their gowns before important events; when they came of age, she saw that they were introduced to marriageable young men. Her interest in Ashton had been even more reserved. She saw that he was fed, clothed, and tutored; she supported whatever discipline Ashton's father felt was required; and she had a servant check on the boy from time to time to ensure that he had not been mislaid or fallen down a well.

"I have never had anything but a sisterly affection for Ashton, but your antipathy rouses my curiosity," Jane said. "I come from a good family. I am well educated. Most of your family like me. Pray tell, what is it about me that you find so objectionable?"

"A single man in possession of a good fortune does not automatically need a wife—not from your class. It is a misconception from which both you and your mother suffer. That we are neighbors and condescend to friendship does not make him your property."

"To be frank, my mother cannot abide your son," Jane said. Mrs. Dennis's physical reaction was an incongruous mix of relief and affront. Jane continued: "And I do not consider any person, male or female, single or married, to be the property of another."

"Noble words to come from the most affected, husband-hunting butterfly I have ever seen!" Mrs. Dennis said. "You are a loose woman. Loose with your thoughts. Loose with your words. Loose with your deeds."

Jane affected a smile, as if Mrs. Dennis had commented favorably upon her dress. She wondered how the world might change if people such as she could say aloud what they really thought and people such as Mrs. Dennis felt restrained enough for silence. There had never been much resemblance between mother and son, but Jane caught it now in the eyes and tight jaw. Rudeness, it appeared, was a humor that passed down to Ashton from both sides of his family. "I beg to differ," Jane replied. "I have never said or done anything without the most careful consideration. That you do not like what I do or say is another matter."

"You bring out the worst in my son. You two are always plotting some misadventure."

Jane laughed. "I have seen Ashton twice in two years!"

"And he is the worse for it each time. He moped around here for a month after the balloon fiasco."

There are women who will rehabilitate from adultery in less time than I will take to live down that damnable balloon ride, Jane thought. "The incident caused my family as many unhappy hours as it did yours. Ashton's mood related to his casting about for ways to make amends. That speaks well of his character—and of the people who raised him."

"Excellent deflection, Miss Austen, but you have neither the wealth nor the disposition to make a suitable wife for the Dennis family."

"*You* married a man when you were penniless."

"Yes, but so was *he*—therein lies the difference. So I must ask, is there an understanding between you and my son?"

"No, there is not."

"Do you comprehend that a marriage between you and my son would be detrimental to his interests?"

"Naturally. Of what service could a decent and honest woman be to a man of wealth?"

"My husband and I worked our way up from poverty to substantial worth," Mrs. Dennis said. "It was not just for us. It was for our family. Ashton likely will double the size of our fortune. You can see that, can you not? His enterprise, his enthusiasm, his understanding of how the world works? Most children of wealth consider it their God-given duty to squander what their parents have earned. It is a rare child of the second generation who will build on what his parents have done. If he marries well, Miss Austen—if he marries *well*—Ashton could become a Member of Parliament. A baronetcy would be inevitable, if not for him then for his son. With the right connections, our family could become one of the most powerful in the country. Our legacy could carry on for a thousand years."

"I have no doubt that Mr. Dennis has the ability and drive to make whatever success he wishes of himself and his life."

"You could set us back two generations, Miss Austen. Indeed, if you had one more litter of deckhands and clergy we would be sunk into oblivion."

"Without the Royal Navy keeping Buonaparte at bay, you would have no wealth. Without the clergy, you would have no civilization."

Mrs. Dennis dismissed this rebuttal with a wave of the hand indicating that neither invasion nor barbarism was the equal of sufficient fortune. "We are not talking about one young man's desires or fancy," she said. "We are talking about the future of an entire family, a matter that is far more important to me than it ever will be to an outsider. ... May I please have your word that you will discourage my son's attentions?"

"I cannot discourage him any more than I already have."

"And decline any offer he should make?"

"You have my word: If he does not ask, I shall not accept."

"Obstinate girl! You refuse to obey the claims of duty, honor, and gratitude. You are determined to ruin him, and me, and his late father—"

"If I am a wild beast, I cannot help it. Ashton prefers me that way."

Jane rose and marched from the room. Hants House was nearly as familiar to her as her childhood home; she took the fastest route to the stables. Learning where the men had gone for the morning, she had a horse saddled for her. Though she had not ridden half a dozen times since she was a child, she set out at a canter. Pockets of fog still hung in the trees like flocks of gray birds too chilled to leave the roost. The sun had risen by now but so lacked animating warmth that it could have been the baleful visage of Mrs. Dennis through the mists.

Jane was not dressed to ride. She wore nothing more substantial than an indoor winter dress and a shawl; her woolen half-gloves left her fingers exposed. It was cold enough crossing the open fields, but upon entering the woods she plowed into a wall of icy air. The path was wide and smooth, but the trees and shrubs were dripping wet. Moisture seemed to condense on her as she rode. The horse's hooves beat the leaves with a frosty crunch. Soon, the horse's breath formed a frosty beard along the sides of its jaws. Her breath, too, blew back and froze on her face.

Fortunately, Ashton and Mr. Fletcher had not ventured far. She found them in a small clearing beside a brook. As she burst from the trees and reined in, she heard some words about whether they would need to reroute the stream. Mr. Fletcher, compact and fit, noticed Jane first, greeting her with a raised eyebrow and the makings of a smile.

The other horse had begun to prance at the sound of her approach, and it took Ashton a few seconds to turn to face her.

"Mr. Dennis, a word?" She pulled out of the hearing of the steward. Ashton joined her. His stallion was on the same scale as he. He was fond of saying that anything under sixteen hands was a pony. "The subject you broached before your mother came in," she said. "I am prepared to give you an answer, one that I hope will meet your satisfaction."

"Then you agree we need a new coach to town?"

"Do not vex me, Mr. Dennis. It is too bitter a day."

"I thought you were unprepared to take a position."

"I hereby waive my disclaimers."

She saw on his face a recognition that matters were approaching finality and a sudden fear that he was unprepared. "This is abrupt, even for me," he said. "Surely, this afternoon, in the comfort of—"

"I am obliged to be back for breakfast in five minutes. I am prepared to leave now, with or without an understanding. According to your wishes."

He hesitated, her comment resonating in some way that tried his memory. She flicked her reins; he grabbed them before her horse could start. The result was that both of their horses circled together.

"You are serious?" he said.

"I have never felt more strongly about any matter in my life."

"D-d-done!" he said.

Chapter 14

Weather has a way of reflecting one's mood. Or rather, one picks from the weather those elements that reinforce one's frame of mind. Jane spent the entire day feeling cold, her spirits soggy. Word spread without a formal announcement. Lady Stanley and Miss Stanley left so abruptly they might have been suspected of absconding with the silver. Mrs. Dennis removed to her room. Though Alethea expressed delight, she was put off by Ashton's reluctance to discuss any details of the courtship. *He* took the first opportunity to leave again with Mr. Fletcher, preferring the gray drizzling damp outdoors to the chill that had settled within. At the end of the day, when Ashton and the remaining ladies dined, no more than the most perfunctory courtesies were expressed. Even the servants were unusually hushed, as if the master had fallen ill rather than in love.

Cassandra came into Jane's room late, as Jane was combing her hair. Cassandra was already prepared for bed. The candle lamp in front of her made her face glow like a religious painting. She put the light on the dresser and sat on the bed. "What a wicked girl," she said. "To carry on a clandestine affair without your older sister having the least suspicion."

"You know very well that there was no affair. I rather wish there had been. It would make sense of matters."

Cassandra said nothing, her lips pursed in anticipation. They had spoken briefly one or two times about the engagement, but their habit was to wait until they were alone before embarking on any meaningful discussions.

"The proposal was a surprise. This morning. At dawn, if you can imagine. He came down while I was playing. I suspect he wanted to ask when he knew his mother could not intervene."

"In the dark, by the fireplace, while you play. How romantic."

"There is nothing quite as romantic as being proposed to by a man half awake, unshaved, and in serious need of a toothbrush." She took out her distaste in the strokes through her hair. "He tried to be sensitive. It is a language he cannot understand."

"You are to be mistress of Hants House! Jane, you are set for life. With sisters-in-law as dear to you as I am."

"And a mother-in-law who thinks I am a fortune hunter."

"Piffle. Ashton will banish her to the Isle of Wight."

They both laughed.

"Have you written to our parents? They will be so proud."

"So relieved."

"Father will dance around his study. Mother will send a messenger instantly to Aunt Perrot."

"I wanted to wait ... before actually writing."

"Ashton cannot change his mind, no matter what pressure his mother might bring upon him. He is a man of his word. And the repercussions if he did withdraw. After everything else—"

"I am thinking of releasing him from his commitment."

Cassandra's recoil and intake of breath were so sharp that the candle guttered in her direction.

"Do you not like him, Jane? I never recognized the seriousness of his attentions, but in retrospect he must care for you acutely."

"I like him well enough. I simply cannot abide his presence."

"Come, he annoys you, but he also makes you smile."

"As a woman smiles at a wayward child. And how will that annoyance be multiplied day after day by the displeasure he takes in everyone and everything? How soon will his rudeness squelch the laughter?"

Cassandra's exasperation was so evident that Jane answered the unasked question.

"It was the surprise. It was all this"—her hands opened to indicate Hants House and all that it represented—"Our future secured! A life of ease and luxury! I said yes out of giddiness. Out of the pleasure it would give our family—and his. And greediness. Cass, Mrs. Dennis may be right." Tears gathered in her eyes. "And vindictiveness."

She told her sister how she had attempted to put off Ashton, how Mrs. Dennis's interruption had resulted in Ashton's departure, and how the woman's vile insults had sent Jane riding furiously after him to accept the proposal before there was any chance of it being withdrawn. "I agreed to the most honorable and personal request a man can make of a woman out of hatefulness and spite."

Cassandra took Jane's hands in hers. "I would never expect a proposal with you to be straightforward. Let us consider the matter logically. Do you care for him?"

"I do not wish to hurt him."

"There must have been some predisposition toward Ashton or you should not have accepted, regardless of Mrs. Dennis's provocations."

"We are all predisposed toward the richest man in Hampshire. That is not a reason to share his bed."

"Do you like him, Jane?"

"There is a ridiculousness about him that entertains me. I daresay he has the same feeling about me."

"Be serious."

"I do not like him as a wife likes a husband." She thought of his roughness, his harsh words. She admitted a prejudice against his stutter—she wanted to call out the words he struggled to speak. He had no taste for literature, for music. If he could not turn it over in his hands, it did not exist for him. "Cass, he has dozed through every evening entertainment."

"He works hard."

"He snores."

"So do you."

"It is bad enough to think of a guest falling asleep at a performance, but how could I possibly compose myself as the hostess?"

"You would thank the performers, bid goodnight to your guests, and gently wake your husband after they had departed."

"How can I love *him*?" Jane said. "We share no interests, no common bonds. What basis do we have for affection? Anything is to be preferred—or endured—rather than marrying without affection."

"Yes," said Cassandra. "But how much affection, and what kind?"

They talked deep into the night. They talked until their voices were as dry as straw, repeating the reasons for and against a number of times. More than once, they changed sides and argued the opposite case. It was their way of ensuring that they explored an issue from every side. Cassandra's words began to mollify the worst of Jane's concerns. Her sister had the right approach: logic. "And can one really know another person during a courtship?" Jane finally said, trying to convince herself. "One might believe she feels affection when it is the flattery of being wooed. One might discover that affection turns to dismay after the marriage vows are said. One might discover that affection was carnality in disguise. Or that a passable friendship is indeed the seed from which love grows."

"I seriously doubt that one can feel any *real* affection beforehand, unless one has known the person for many years," Cassandra said. "Mother says there is no comparison between her feelings before her marriage and afterward. Working together and living together are bound to increase one's respect and love of the other party."

"It is an argument made in so very many different ways by women aspiring to raise themselves in life," Jane said. "Because one cannot know ahead of time, one might as well swoon over a rich man as a poor one. Which, it appears, I have managed to do."

"The odds of success—of happiness—are equally good," Cassandra said.

"Single women have a terrible propensity for being poor," Jane said. "No one has to convince me of the value of marrying well. I insist only that there must be a foundation of endearment to every commitment." Here, logic failed. "I like Ashton, but he is not dear to me. I cannot imagine that he ever will be."

"Jane," Cassandra said, attempting still again to drag her from the brambles of recklessness and scandal onto the path of prudence and practicality. "No one wants you to commit to man you abhor, but—"

"And what of Father?" Jane asked suddenly. She pulled his letter out of her writing desk and reminded Cass of the closing passage. "See how he warns that *immaturity* can lead to *hasty decisions* bearing *long-term consequences.*"

"His admonition against hasty action more likely applies to rescinding an engagement than to accepting a *legitimate* offer of *marriage.* From a good man." Cass emphasized the words in the same frantic tone that Jane had used to emphasize hers, highlighting the ludicrousness of Jane's interpretation of their father's counsel.

Cassandra's last words sent Jane's mind into a dizzying spin. She spoke vehemently, as if her summary had to rebut all of her sister's guidance during the long night. "I cannot do it," she said. "I have misled him. I cannot say if his feelings for me are those of a boy or man, but I have no doubt that they are real. You should have seen his face when I accepted. He believes I share his affections. That is the worst betrayal any woman could ever exact on a man. Ashton's kind of fondness leads naturally to the obligations of marriage." She paused before concluding: "His hands, Cass! I can never imagine those monstrous slabs of meat on my person!"

Chapter 15

Jane found Ashton in the library after breakfast the next day. She paused, as she usually did, to admire the books. One section held more volumes than her father's entire substantial collection at Steventon. She could almost imagine becoming Ashton's wife for the sole benefit of spending her life in this room. Just as she could almost imagine becoming his wife to obtain the luxurious house, the servants to wait on her every whim, the acres of carefully appointed gardens and woods, the Greek ruin. The operative word was *almost*. She made her way slowly down one side, caressing the leather bindings as she went. This could well be the last time she would venture here. In the few niches that did not contain books were paintings of gentlemen with hunting dogs and gentlemen with horses. A globe was strategically set on a stand on one side of the desk and a telescope on the opposite side near the window. The placements were designed to create an impression of considered thought, as though there were a scholar at the desk who routinely spun the globe while considering matters that would affect the entire world, one who used the telescope to examine nature in the minutest detail. As with the rest of the house, which was covered with paintings of ancestors of every important family in England *except* the newly wealthy Dennises, this room was intended to create a sense of substance and history that might—*if Ashton married well*—become the truth a generation hence. Mrs. Dennis used the art of home decorating to anticipate, if not directly influence, the future.

Today's occupant of the desk, however, contradicted the perception of the scholar in contemplative thought or (projected forward) of the wealthy squire confidently maneuvering his children's lives for posterity's sake. Ashton's desk was weighed down with contracts, reports, and letters. He went through them searching for a document, cursing with a bitterness that other men might reserve for a serious loss of revenue. When she interrupted, he scowled as if she were another bill to pay.

"Why do housemaids come without wits?" he asked. "I tell them over and over, do not move anything on my desk. Do not clean my desk. Stay away from my desk. I come down to find that they have *tidied*, causing me half an hour's delay to un-tidy things into stacks I can make sense of."

"Probably because they are lectured by your mother if they do *not* put everything in order. Regrettably, she is far more frightening than you."

Abandoning his search, Ashton came around the desk, picked her up by both arms, spun her around him like a doll, and kissed her as sloppily as a mastiff. "We are to be married, Jane! Married!"

"Ashton! A little decorum, please. I am not your plaything."

"But you are, Jane." He leaned in and whispered to her. "And there's nothing anyone can do to keep us from playing now!"

"Put me down."

"Yes, Miss Austen."

She found a distance close enough that they could talk quietly but far enough that she could avoid another lunge.

"Ashton, things have happened so rapidly that I believe we should take a moment to catch our breath. You yourself feared that our actions were too *abrupt*. I forced you to make a declaration in haste."

"You expected me to keep my word."

"You had not actually *given* your word. That is the point. I forced you to give it prematurely under the pressure of an ultimatum. And my motivations were not as pure as yours."

"You would not have said yes for the wrong reasons."

"I am ashamed to say that your circumstances, and the security they offer, greatly mattered in my answer. I was overcome at the prospect of being mistress of Hants House. Even more grievously, I compelled your engagement in order to gain revenge against your mother."

"There are worse reasons to marry. No doubt she deserved it." He moved behind his desk to sit, as if they had settled the concerns about which she had come to speak.

"Your mother made the most horrible accusations against my character. I have never been angrier in my life. My acceptance did not stem from affection for you but from my own selfishness and anger.

No marriage should begin in this manner. I cannot—will not—hold you to your promise."

"I do not ask that you release me."

"Surely ..."

"We have an agreement, Jane. Whatever the details of the negotiations, I have no quarrel with the outcome."

"You cannot be insensitive to an agreement based on fraudulent motives. A contract, founded in fraud or error, is of no effect."

"I am utterly insensitive. I have you, and that is all I want."

Seeing that disengagement was going to require more finesse than she had imagined, Jane settled into the steward's chair. She did not know precisely what to say.

"Given the hostility of your mother, and the suddenness of events, perhaps it would be best to wait before we formalize our relationship," Jane suggested. "I fear that the haste of our actions may lend credence to suppositions about our behavior earlier. That it was inappropriate."

"I do not give a tinker's damn about others' suppositions. You and I know very well—we did nothing wrong."

"In society, more truth is given to appearance than reality."

"That is society's problem, not mine."

Ask me again, she thought. *Nicely.* The idea came as a surprise, as had her words a few seconds earlier when she suggested a delay, rather than a cancellation, of their engagement. She put on her most pleasant face. "Let us return to where we were in the morning before your mother interrupted. Let us see where the conversation leads. So that neither one of us ever has cause to regret either the substance or the manner of our agreement."

Jane understood now what she had for months kept out of mind. She had suspected at some level that Ashton would propose. He had found so many ways to be in her presence, over such a period of time, that an offer became almost inevitable. Yet he had never expressed the courtesies that any woman would wish to hear—even if she expected to disregard them. Even yesterday morning he had wanted her to guess his intent and give him an answer before he asked! (Which, indeed, she had done.) To her, a proposal should be a dance of words. She hoped to glide toward the outcome and away two or three times, lightly circling the sweet topic before their momentum swept them to a pleasing conclusion. *However briefly, she wanted to be wooed.* All she required to become Ashton's wife was to see some grace in this storm of a young man.

"Jane, it is done. I am busy." He pointed to the multiple stacks of paper, each a foot high. "Feel free to talk with Alethea and Cassandra about dates, times, details. I will be happy with whatever you decide."

"I am not a piece of furniture with the only question being where to place me in your house."

He slammed his fist on the desk, causing her to jump.

"I gave you my word. You gave me yours. What more? What's on your mind? Be brief. Be honest. I have ten hours of work to do in three hours' time."

Jane fairly leapt from the chair. "Ashton, in a word—no!"

"No?"

"I regret that I must withdraw my acceptance of your kind proposal. I agreed to marry you under false pretenses. I will not be false with you now."

He flinched as if slapped. He recovered and stood, rising like a mountain before her.

"Forgive me," she said. "I do not mean to be rude. I do not mock your admonition to make the answer short—if not sweet. I am sincerely trying to be as forthright with you as you have been with me."

"Y-your s-straightforwardness is noted."

Her rejection, she realized, was brutal precisely because it was sincere. Whatever brief thought she had had of saying yes evaporated like dew on a hot day. If he could show any subtlety, any tendency toward the finer emotions, any sense of pace and decorum, of a lady's desire for, if not fine words then tender feelings ... if only ... then ... perhaps ... perhaps. That was not Ashton. Even if he were to drop on bended knee to plead, he would blurt out his proposal with all the finesse of a bid at a livestock auction.

"Your generosity made me believe I could love you," she said. "Who could not love your sisters, or the security you offer? I am proud enough—vain enough—to have given you the answer you wished. Every woman is foolish when it comes to proposals. But today I must give you the honest answer you deserve to hear. I hope you will forgive me."

"Why would you induce me to send off Miss Stanley, a woman who was perfect for me, if not to have me for yourself?"

"I can care for your future happiness, without being the source of it."

"C-can I m-make it any p-plainer that I care for you?"

"I believe you sincerely desire to protect my honor from all of the terrible aspersions to which I have been subjected," she said. "You impulsively act out of kindness without understanding the longer-term consequences. But if you search inside yourself you will see that you are as motivated to prove society wrong—*and your mother*—as I was. This is no reason to marry."

"Why do you presume to know my feelings? Trust me to tell you what they are!"

"You are a man. You do not have feelings until a woman describes them to you."

"Men are not so clever as women," he said forlornly. "We are capable of saying only what we mean."

His remark made her pause, but only for a moment. He did not claim to be a gentleman, nor did she care about that word in the sense of sophisticated gentility. Indeed, overly genteel males made her skin crawl. She was not certain, however, that someone with his enthusiasm was a gentle *man*, a *gentle* man. It was unsuitable somehow for a person to discharge so much energy. She was afraid that his electricity might strike her dead, or exhaust her in the daily interchange of marriage. Nor could she imagine sitting year after year by the fire with someone who found pleasure only in the field and office, in the work of the hand and body and the practical demands of the mind.

Married or no, her life's work was the work of the intellect. She could make do, of course. She could accept the duties of marriage—all of them—with woman's natural ability to deal patiently with whatever life required of her. She bore a responsibility to relieve herself, her mother, and her sister of the slow decline of prosperity that awaited them once their father died. She had no desire to measure out her existence, as so many spinsters did, by hoarding her pennies for firewood. But she would *not* make do. It was no more in her nature to make do on the matter of her heart than it was for Ashton to appreciate any of the fine paintings that anointed the walls around him. And she knew that Ashton would not wish her to *make do*. He would, in truth, take offense at the idea anyone would *make do* by marrying him.

As these thoughts roiled her brain, he stewed. "You cannot turn me down!" he said, suddenly and explosively. "It is insolence—someone of your station rejecting this opportunity."

She saw that his remark was from wounded rather than excessive pride, but she was unable to withhold her response. "My station is no lower than that of your parents when they were my age."

"Unlike them you are not certain to raise yourself—except through me."

"I find it curious that the greatest admonitions to raising one's self in life come from men who have had everything handed to them."

"I do more work in a day than you do in a week."

"To consolidate your wealth and control over others. Even when you help people, it seems to be for the purpose of reminding them of your power to do so."

"Poverty is no measure of character."

"One is likely to find more honest men in the work house than in the House of Lords. Your power and position do not make you a better man. Your advantages were given, not earned."

"My primary advantage is to be shrewder—and work harder—than other men. This does not speak so well of me as it does badly of them. Most men are either excessively stupid or excessively lazy. A surprising number are both. Including a few in your family."

"You need to enlarge your soul, Mr. Dennis. If your spiritual nature should ever grow to fit the magnitude of your body and your conceit, you would be a man to reckon with."

"This is the estimation in which you hold me! Thank you for explaining it so well."

He came toward her and loomed over her against the edge of her chair. For an instant she was frightened. Then he seemed to collapse like the balloon after the crash. In an instant, he lost half his physical space.

"Have you ever felt *anything*, Jane? You talk too well to feel so very deeply. ... Have you ever had respect, honest regard, genuine affection? For a man. Ever?"

"My heart is not closed, Mr. Dennis. I feel as much as any human feels. Affection, hope, love. Anger, despair, doubt. ... Do not confuse modest speech with modest feelings."

"My speech is proportional to my feelings. If yours is inverse, then you must feel very deeply toward me."

She could not entirely repress her laugh. "I cannot enter into any arrangement without the warmest of feelings for my intended," she says. "That is all a lady should ever have to feel—or say!"

"I would care for you and your family," he said, his voice strangely choked. "You would have everything you want. Anything. Always. ... I will ask *precious* little."

"Why do you force me to be cruel? A promise of security will not induce me to change my mind. Nothing can be compared to the misery of being bound without love."

He straightened to his full height. "Miss Austen, if you were susceptible to blandishment, we should all be disappointed. But blandishment is the only thing I have left. You are a rare woman. You do not want me. *Or* my wealth."

"I regret to say that I do not."

"Look at me, Jane. I c-could make y-you happy."

She returned his gaze, though her voice wavered. "No, you could not. Our *friendship* is very dear to me. That is why I speak such dreadful words." She realized how much this friendship did mean to her. Had she made a terrible mistake—was it too late to change her decision, to tell him that she would accept his offer after all? Yet he stood before her, all mass and misproportion. An image came to mind of him sleeping through a sonata: All of the friendship in the world could not overcome their divide. She rose and touched his face. "You will try. I know you will try your utmost. And that is the tragedy. You will do everything you can to make me love you, and I will not. In the end, I will resent your insistence, and you will despise me for my failure to return your love."

"I could never despise you."

"Then you will spend your life despising yourself. You will hold yourself a failure for giving everything to me and receiving nothing in return. I cannot bear the thought of you enduring the perpetual sadness of a marriage without love."

"But you can bear the thought of me being alone, away from the one woman I ... w-wish ... to ... b-be with."

"The only person unhappier than a woman who does not love her husband is the husband who must live with her."

"I wish you had less wisdom and more affection," he said.

"And you less affection and more—" She stopped, mortified.

"No, you are right." He waved his hand, signaling that he would not importune her further. "Thank you for your consideration," he said. "Your candor."

They stood facing each other. He seemed now spent, rocking back and forth like an animal that has raced until its legs are lost. She could feel her own heat, anger, frustration, embarrassment. We must look as though we have spent the last five minutes pummeling one another, she thought: For of course they very much had.

"Mr. Dennis, I must ask you never to bring up the subject of marriage again. It is too painful for both of us."

When he did not respond, she insisted that he give his word.

In the stilted tones of a person taking an unpleasant oath, he said: "I promise I will never again broach the subject of marriage to Miss Jane Austen."

They were done, yet neither of them wished to part. It was as though they needed to reestablish their old equilibrium, or at least some new emotional interchange at a lower level of intensity than what they had just experienced.

"The house will be in an uproar," he said. "You must leave."

"Of course."

"Alethea may be more disappointed than I."

"I offend everyone I care about here, and delight the one I do not."

"Mother will glory in her triumph."

"One does what one can to brighten an old woman's day."

"I do not wish you subject to her malice. ... Go. Now."

He returned to his desk and sprawled into the chair. This was the only time she ever remembered seeing him in a posture of defeat. He turned toward her with his scraped rock of a face. His eyes were so dark and impenetrable she could not tell whether he remained angry or hurt. She saw how terribly close he came to being handsome.

Part II

Winter 1802-Summer 1805

Chapter 16

---

16 December 1802

Dearest Alethea

The occasion of my birthday reminds me of all the joy and good companions I have in my life, including you and your family. Every day since our departure from Hants House I have had reason to appreciate the good-heartedness you showed in accompanying us to Steventon. I have waited to express my thanks for fear that too early a letter might inflame the feelings of some in your household; yet I do not want to wait too long for fear you should consider me ungrateful.

Without your company, our removal would have resembled a rout. As it was, we might have pretended to be off on a quiet coach ride instead of fleeing from the well-deserved wrath of your family. Your presence helped mitigate the anguish we felt over the hurt we had caused. I say "we" because it is automatic to use that term when Cassandra and I are together. It is so much easier to pretend that someone else shared in the responsibility— though Cassy, once again, was simply along for the ride.

Your decision to join us must have led to a chill—if not an outright winter storm—upon your return to Hants House. I do not mean with Ashton, who I suspect drew comfort from our discreet leave-taking rather than from the debacle it might have been. Indeed, perhaps the general sense may have been one of relief. Did Mrs. Dennis feel anger at my insult to her family or joy that Ashton was free again to pursue a better match? I suspect your mother has the capacity to feel both emotions simultaneously.

It was good that you and Catherine left the rectory promptly. Though we did not discuss the cause of our unscheduled return—or of our insistence that James deliver us immediately to Bath—the haste of our business left Mary quite unhappy. She must have believed we were fleeing a smallpox *epidemic. Because of the length of the journey, James had to hire another clergyman to preach in his absence. I do not know whether Mary's alarm was the result of the cost of James' replacement or of her not having access to the reason. Let her be peevish. My business is not hers. Even after a year, I remain peevish with her for having obtained all of our library for not a third of what the books were worth.*

The proceedings at Bath were more subdued than you might have expected. While I sat in the bedroom, waiting to be called for the summary trial and execution, Cassandra explained all that had happened to Mother and Father. There was no uproar. I heard the door close to Father's study. I heard the door close to Mother's bedroom. Cass came to our room. We undressed in silence. The next few days were the quietest that one could ever experience in an Austen household.

It was not an angry silence but a sad one, as if we had lost a dear friend under tragic circumstances. I suppose we have.

I hope the Christmas season, which is always so busy and bright at Hants House, relieves the distress of this dreary, misty month of December. Quiet will reign here for some time to come. Do let me know how things go.

Y^{rs} very affec.^{ly}
Jane

—————

9 January 1803

Dearest Alethea

Normally I can expect to hear from you within a day or two by return Post. I must hope that you have been busy over Christmas.

Alethea, I know by your comportment that you understand the grief in my heart over my rejection of Ashton's too generous proposal. In searching my own heart, I could not find an emotion equivalent to his. It is wretched that I must wound him now to avoid wounding him more deeply if we had become bound together as husband and wife. We should not have to be hurtful in order to be truthful, but that is the harsh choice that life sometimes presents.

I would rather be ridiculed by society as the silly woman who turned away an advantageous situation than be reviled by Ashton—by you!—as the horrid woman who made him miserable. Dear boy. If only he were not so young. Or I, not so old.

Perhaps it is good that I disrupted things so thoroughly between us all. Neither Ashton nor I will be in a position to converse, which is where the trouble starts. We do not flirt. Indeed, there never was any hint of romance. But there is an odd charm to the way in which we disagree. We tantalize each other into seeking the reform of our antagonist. Or perhaps we simply enjoy annoying someone we respect.

I conclude, my dear friend, by offering my love to you and my friendship to Ashton. I know he will find someone more suited to his needs and more grateful for his open heart. Please write as soon as you can.

Y.ʳˢ very affec.ˡʸ
Jane

—∾⦿⦿⦿∾—

23 January 1803

Dearest Alethea

I am beyond worry at not having received a letter. Have you decided on reflection that I am too hateful to be considered? Can you not forgive my actions? You know my love for you. You know my regard for Ashton, even if I cannot offer him more. I understand if you never wish to see me—or if your family insists that you do not—but I cannot bear your silence and all that it implies. If we are never to communicate again, at least let us end with a declaration of affection and friendship. Or of confidence. Something that lets me know you do not hate me.

Y.ʳˢ in distress,
Jane

—∾⦿⦿⦿∾—

26 January 1803

Jane

Ashton is gone. Madness here. More soon.

Y.ʳˢ,
Alethea

⸺ܥܘܣܘܥܣܘ ⸺

3 February 1803

Dear Sister

Here is the news, directly from Alethea: Ashton has set sail on a British ship of the line for the West Indies. He left with little notice. Everything has fallen on Alethea's shoulders. I will get as far as I can on the matter before she calls for me again.

It was strange to come off the coach from Bath in such haste and agitation. It was like our last trip except in reverse. James and Mary had heard the news about Ashton at Steventon but felt it best that we should hear directly from the Dennises. Upon my arrival, James sent a note to Alethea, knowing she would have me come to her immediately. There I learned the full story.

As you know, Ashton likes an unusual guest list for dinner. You will recall that one of our dinners included a young naval lieutenant, the one with the thin face, bushy brows, and scar over the right eye—he slurred his r's. He and Ashton became friends. After we left, the lieutenant returned a number of times, diverting Ashton with tales of the sea. At the last dinner, it became understood that the lieutenant had room on his ship for a gentleman passenger to the West Indies and that Ashton was desirous of joining him. The more excited the conversation became, the more difficult it was for any words to be articulated. Between Ashton's stutter and the lieutenant's r's, it took half of the first course for one exchange of dialogue. Or so Alethea reported.

Before the men retired for brandy, they had agreed that Ashton would ship out with the lieutenant as an informal member of the crew to study whatever has not been studied on tropic isles. When Mrs. Dennis remonstrated at the idea of her son going off on an ocean voyage, Ashton told her that it had always been his dream to be a natural philosopher. He wants to venture the world in search of new species of flora and fauna like Sir Joseph Banks in Tahiti. In an effort to dissuade them, Mrs. Dennis fainted multiple times, but in their eagerness to plot the adventure they practically stepped over her body, as if she were an old tree that had fallen in the forest. (Quoting Alethea again.)

You must thank your instincts, Jane, whatever they were that caused you to separate yourself from Ashton as you did. Who could believe he *would be so unpredictable? I cannot bear the thought of his traveling to that horrid part of the world.*

More later—

Y*ʳˢ very affec.ˡʸ*
Cass

—⁓⁓•⊙⊙⊙⊙•⁓⁓—

9 February 1803

Dear Jane

Cassandra has written to you about Ashton's departure. I am grateful that she did. I have been too busy to arrange my thoughts. Frankly, I did not know what explanation to offer. I recognized that your denial of him might have played a part in his decision to go—"the only victory over love is flight"—but he assures me that this is not the case.

I asked him directly whether the broken engagement had any part in his decision. He laughed. "Jane was right," he said, with no further explanation. Until then, he had been brooding, but now he really seemed fine—liberated to pursue his own interests. I understood his desire for adventure, but I know he feels too much responsibility to the family to simply run off. I asked his real reason for leaving. He gave me a reply unlike anything I ever expected to hear from our practical Little Brother. "I must enlarge my soul," he said.

More later—

Y*ʳˢ very affec.ˡʸ*
Alethea

—⁓⁓•⊙⊙⊙⊙•⁓⁓—

14 February 1803

Dearest Alethea

I cannot imagine what was going on in Ashton's mind. To leave Hampshire, to abandon Hants House and all its holdings and businesses, to pursue the study of natural history in a disease-infested part of the world!?!? (Normally I insist on just one punctuation mark per emotion but such a sentence compels additional strokes.) To do something this unbelievable! It is just like a young man, governed by the whim of the moment, or actuated merely by the love of doing anything oddly!

I am sorry that Cassy was the first in our family to hear the news. I fear that she will worry endlessly because of what happened to her Tom in San Domingo. I hope my mentioning Tom does not incite worry in your heart for Ashton.

Your brother's tutors at Oxford said he was interested in everything new and shiny but had no more ability to sustain his attention than a puppy. Henry relayed this intelligence some months ago. It will be a terrible thing if Ashton is on a cramped ship in the middle of the ocean when he discovers he would rather be galloping across a field at home.

In eager expectation of hearing more,

Jane

—————

21 February 1803

Dear Sister

There is not much to add about Ashton's departure. Dr. Herschel made most of the arrangements, gathering expeditionary clothing and technical equipment, evidently with the enthusiastic support of Sir Joseph Banks of the Royal Society. Sir Joseph is determined to send every able-bodied man in England, who is not otherwise engaged, to study caterpillars and crustaceans in every part of the world.

And there was the settling of all the family concerns before he sailed with his lieutenant on the next tide. Mr. Fletcher can run the farm, naturally, but there are a dozen men involved in the different enterprises in Hampshire, Kent, and London. Ashton is no fool about business. He left firm instructions on how each is to be run and made arrangements for receiving regular reports once he is established. He has lawyers and finance men watching the business men and a second set of lawyers and finance men watching the first. According to Alethea, they creep around like funeral directors hoping for someone to drop dead.

Ashton also charged Alethea with making regular and unannounced visits to every establishment. This was highly objectionable to the directors. The prevailing wisdom, of course, is that a woman should never be trusted with money. But a look or word made them understand that they are to treat her as they would treat Ashton—or they would meet with Ashton's wrath upon his return. Mr. Jarrett, who handles the import-export company, was particularly uncooperative until Ashton dangled him out the window by his collar. Well, perhaps it wasn't entirely out the window, but Alethea said it was enough that the breeze ruffled Mr. Jarrett's hair.

Fortunately, Alethea has regularly reviewed the ledgers as a check on Ashton whenever he was pressed for time. I do not believe that she has the broad view of the enterprises that Ashton does, but she can balance to the farthing where he cannot. "There will not be so much as a grain of wheat pilfered under my watch," she said. The headstrong nature of the Dennis clan is of great value today.

Y* sister,
Cassandra

———⌇⌇⌇⌇⌇⌇⌇———

22 February 1803

Dear Jane

Tonight is the first night that I do not have a long list of worries. I look forward to writing to you without haste. Cassy and I talk several times a day. I know that she has fully apprised you of Ashton's leaving; indeed, I asked her to send you the details of my being handed the responsibility for the farm and businesses. She has described to you the confidence my brother felt in our operations, as well as the safeguards he put in place.

Perhaps most important, my father and Ashton have done well by these men, so they have every incentive to do well by us in my brother's absence. Even Mr. Jarrett is a good man at heart, just rather more traditional than required at this moment.

The real cross to bear is Mother. She is convinced that our family fortune will evaporate in Ashton's absence. Or drown with him in the sea. (I suppose the latter is possible, since he is the only heir.) She is of the belief that money must be kept in full and constant view or it will disappear like dew in the morning sun. She has taken to reading the financial pages of the newspapers whenever she can. When the market is down, she takes this as proof of our doom. When the market is up, she is certain that the rise will end in collapse. We have seven businesses in total. She has set her calendar to worry about each one on successive *days. I told her even God rested on the seventh day, but she is convinced that the Sabbath requires her to sit at the window and sob over the price of cotton.*

I wish I could send her off to an elderly friend with whom she could commiserate over the foolishness of youth, but Mother has accumulated no friends. To her, friends are as inconvenient as a collection of porcelain dolls, except that she cannot assign a maid to dust them off.

In rereading your letters, I realize I never answered your most tender question. Yes, my dear Jane, I still love you. It is my brother who remains my chief exasperation.

Yrs very affec.[y]
Alethea

Chapter 17

----

24 February 1803

Dear Charles

I hope the winds and tides and naval efficiency bring this letter to you promptly. Father and Mother are both well. Father's health is steadfast. Cass and I enjoy the doings of Bath society.

I wish to ask a favor. You are aware, of course, of some of the events surrounding Mr. Ashton Dennis of Hants House in Hampshire. Mr. Dennis recently undertook a scientific expedition to the British West Indies. Indeed, he may have already arrived in Barbados. He is traveling aboard a British warship, very likely destined to travel from island to island.

Mr. Dennis and I had a misunderstanding shortly before his voyage, and I was not able to fully set things right before he left. I have enclosed a message for him in the hope that you might find a way to deliver it. The urgency of the matter, and my desire that Mr. Dennis not carry unpleasant feelings for the year or more that he will be absent, make it imperative that I reach him.

I thought you would be more likely to relay my correspondence than Frank, as you are aware of more of the background, and perhaps can understand better the importance of our maintaining friendly relations with the Dennis family. If the message comes from you, rather than directly from me, I feel certain that we will have obeyed the dictates of discretion.

The entire family sends their love and best wishes.

Yʳ loving sister,
Jane

24 February 1803

Dear Mr. Dennis

If you are not the death of yourself, you will be the death of me. Expand your soul? It is rather more likely that you have lost your mind. I doubt that you will find it in the West Indies. If something should happen to you, in addition to the grief that we all would feel, I should forever be haunted by guilt. I would never again be able to face your sisters, who are my dearest friends. Nor your mother, who commands my respect and consideration if not my affection.

It is so like you to take an intemperate remark by a frustrated woman and turn it into one of the Commandments. How is that supposed to make me feel? Am I to be impressed by a hasty, ill-considered decision that takes you across the sea into dangerous climes? Cassandra is quite beside herself. You must recall that her fiancé died there, on a mission a good deal less self-absorbed than yours.

You reel from brilliance to fool-hardiness like a pendulum clock. My father remarked that such inconsistency is the mark of a man who has not yet found himself. I pray that you find yourself on this voyage and that you do so quickly. I do not mean to be harsh in my admonition. It is anguish, not anger, that fuels my pen. Come home safe to your family and friends. And soon!

Sincerely,
J. Austen

―⁓⦿⦾⦿⁓―

12 April 1803

Dear Sister

You may be surprised to learn that the British fleet does not huddle all together at Barbados like carriages in Covent Garden. Nor are the many islands of the West Indies as close as Steventon and Basingstoke. However, the seafaring community in the North American Station is small, and I have been able to direct your letter to a kindly officer and friend. He, in turn, found the vessel on which Mr. Dennis now serves—or lives aboard, as I am not certain of his status. The letter has been forwarded to Mr. Dennis on a dispatch ship.

As far as he and the Admiralty are concerned, this is correspondence from one member of the British contingent to another. Considering Mr. Dennis's services to the Austen family, I have no trouble whatsoever in assisting communication from any of us. In my own note, I offered whatever services he might need should our ships cross paths. As you know, I am being considered for my own command. The rumor is that I may be posted to Bermuda. I shall watch for our Mr. Dennis. After the rain and cold of England, he must find the Caribbean a pleasant region. My friend says that, if it were not for the hurricanes, the insects, the disease, the French, and the Spanish, it would be Paradise.

You were wise to make the request of me rather than of my sailing brother.

Y^r *loving brother,*
Charles
HMS Endymion
At sea

———————

5 May 1803

Dear Miss Austen

I received your letter and your good wishes thanks to your brother Charles. He displays the Austen ingenuity in locating me.

Let me discourage any apprehensions about my voyage.

If I do not need to expand my soul, I need to expand my mind. If I have lost my mind, I do indeed hope to retrieve it here.

For you to judge a matter correctly does not make you responsible for the matter. Or for the actions required to set the matter right. Also, beyond my own reasons for setting out, I needed Alethea to take responsibility for Hants House and the other family enterprises. I have full confidence in her abilities, but she requires direct experience to develop the assurance needed for herself. Never doubt that the Dennis holdings will remain my primary concern. But I also must have the freedom to leave from time to time.

I recognize the irregularity of asking a woman to manage financial concerns. It is another of the insanities of our time. A female aristocrat, unmarried or widowed, can take charge of her huge estate, the poorest woman in the village can run a shop. Yet a practical woman of the other ranks of society is not allowed to help in her family's business simply because "it is not done." In the Dennis family, it will be done. On Hants as it is in Heaven. I have no hesitation in using everything in my power to ensure that Alethea is listened to. If the artifice is that she is acting on my behalf, rather than using her own judgment, then so be it. To use her own judgment is to act on my behalf. I trust her completely. I will reckon up all accounts upon my return—in every way that is necessary with the men who work for me. They understand my intent.

I do not expect to make natural history the occupation of my life. But I do need something to escape the tedium of the daily management of business. I cannot tell you how often my eyes cross in exhaustion over farm and business inventories or the prices of sheep and crops. And I have been responsible for my family's affairs for barely two years. ... I cannot imagine how I would feel after forty. It is only the ability to ride in the open air to carry out most of my business that has kept me sane at all. You prefer to walk. But I believe we benefit from the same salutary effects of Nature. By the time Alethea's eyes begin to cross, I hope I shall have returned. For now, she is relishing the novelty. Knowing my sister, she will enjoy her work to the extent that it taxes her. The more she fusses over the Dennis concerns, the happier she will be.

On our journey to the Caribbean, we had the opportunity to make stops at several American ports of call. One cannot imagine the frantic nature of America. The towns are ripped from the wilderness. Everyone has a plan—a scheme. There is no such thing as a leisurely pace. Everyone is behind. People hop off a ship and head inland with nothing more than a musket and a horse. The atmosphere is so contagious that one is tempted to join them ... but there is only so far that even I am willing to push my beloved mother.

The West Indies have so far proved to be everything I might have wished. The seas, the skies, the amazing creatures. I do not know whether I can maintain the steady dispassion required of a natural philosopher. I am like a boy given a roomful of new playthings. After visiting only two islands, I had already filled several boxes with specimens.

Even if you have exhausted your admonitions, it would not be unpleasant to hear from you again. Letters are few and far between. Though the duties of Hants House can be tedious, the many sounds of a large household also provide comfort. Here, the silence that stimulates the mind also accentuates the isolation.

Write care of Mr. Jarrett at our firm in Southampton. If you include a thought on whatever you may read of industry or science, we can treat the communication as "business." It would be no different than if I wrote Miss Caroline Herschel about observations from this part of the world, as I would do without hesitation if I had the necessary astronomical skills. Such objective correspondence would not violate any protocol. A protocol that, however ludicrous, I know that you will feel constrained to observe.

Sincerely,
A. Dennis
Barbados
North American Station

P.S. Your father is correct.

———————◦◦◦◦◦◦◦———————

15 June 1803

Dearest Cassandra

I am uncertain as to whether I should respond to the wishes of the enclosed letter and correspond with Mr. Dennis. I fear that a response might encourage feelings that must be laid quietly to rest. Or, if our correspondence were to become known, it might set tongues to wagging yet again, however much related to business the contents of such letters might be.

At the same time, there is his latest favor to us involving Henry and Eliza, not to mention the isolation of which he speaks, though I suspect the "isolation" will include many pleasant interludes. How likely is it that Mr. Dennis would maintain feelings for me when he finds himself for months, if not years, in an alien community with marriageable women from good families who desperately want to come to England? It is well known that the region has a large supply of eligible young ladies and few men of sufficiently desirable wealth or reputation. Nelson's wife and Buonaparte's Josephine both hail from the Caribbean! No, there is more than enough feminine bounty in the Indies to distract Mr. Dennis from an impecunious spinster back home.

Duty, not to mention courtesy, requires that I answer him, if only to express thanks for his aid with H and E. Do you not agree?

Y^r *loving sister,*
Jane

⁓∽◦⚬⊙⚬◦∽⁓

15 June 1803

Dear Mr. Dennis

 Having me serve as the intermediary between you and science is akin to having a deaf person offer a critique of classical music. What I know of natural history is limited to a passing article in a newspaper, which may be more along the lines of the birth of a two-headed calf than the age of the stars or the composition of the Earth.

 However, like clockwork, the Austen family has again fallen into your debt, so I shall endeavor to repay with my pen what you have paid in service. You obviously knew of Henry and Eliza's plans to travel to France to seek to recover the property of her late first husband. Or at least to recover the money that Eliza and her mother had put into the Comte's estate. Unfortunately, when arrested during the Terror the Comte confessed not only to theft but to murder. *He must have believed that admitting a level of brutality equal to that of his captors might spare him the guillotine. Instead, he lost his head and Eliza lost any hope of recourse.*

 The war resumed before Henry and Eliza could return home. Fortunately, Eliza speaks better French than Buonaparte. She had Henry wrapped up like an invalid inside their carriage—carrying the plague, the sentries believed, based on her artful deception. No one dared go near him. Masquerading as a French couple, they were able to reach the coast and find a ship home. Safely back in England, they told me that it was you who had, well in advance, arranged safe passage aboard a trading vessel. The Austens must cease falling into bankruptcy and war or we shall never be free of our obligations to you.

 From the London newspapers and letters from Miss Herschel, I can give you the news that Mr. Davy continues to lecture everywhere. I remember you and Dr. Herschel discussing his work at one of the dinners. Mr. Davy believes chemistry is at the heart of everything in the world. After hearing your discourse with Dr. Herschel and reading of Mr. Davy's work, I confess that when I see flowers growing in the field I sense a bit more of what is happening—out of sight—as it were. It does not dispel my enjoyment of the world's beauty to know that it rests on some chemical incantation. Rather it enhances my belief in God's mysteries to know that such bounty comes from minute and complex sequences that only He could have created.

If Mr. Davy has a flaw, it is that he proselytizes chemistry with the zeal of a Methodist evangelical. He promises salvation through careful logic and experimentation. The "carbon cycle" is to be the New Testament. One would think that chemical processes constitute the soul. I find such thinking sterile, as if human beings were nothing but little bags of compounds mixed together at an alchemist's table. It makes one wonder at how his mind might have been affected by his gas experiments. I am sure you are aware of the gossip attached to his inhalation therapies. I must give the Devil his due, however. Albemarle Street has become the first one-way street in London so that Mr. Davy's adherents may get to his lectures promptly.

At home we are again on a war footing. We seem to have everything necessary to carry on the conflict except an unlimited supply of young men. The recruiters are out in force, and the prices being paid for substitutes are increasing every week—from ten guineas to five and forty! My brother James is helping raise a Corps of Volunteers—to supplement the regular Army and the Militia—as part of the government's effort to create a home force large enough to dissuade Buonaparte from invasion. Frank and Charles in the Navy, James and Henry, once in the Militia and now expecting to serve as Volunteers: That accounts for all the men in the family! There is talk that the force may be as large as two or three hundred thousand volunteers. There is also talk of levies to raise an actual Army of Reserve—but laborers cannot afford to leave their work and farmers cannot afford to leave their fields. (And the Army needs farmers to remain where they are because soldiers require food every bit as much as ordinary citizens.) It is unclear whether the levies will be able to bring in enough paid soldiers to make the effort worthwhile, because potential recruits fear that, once in the Army, they will be sent overseas. Volunteers, therefore—training in their spare time—seem to be the only solution, as they obviously can serve only to protect our homes and people. James says his men are showing good progress (though James, himself no soldier, may not be qualified to speak). My brother Frank, who is responsible for the defenses along the Kent coast, has a less optimistic view of such corps, which seem to comprise men too old, too young, or too infirm to be of much value. He calls the typical sea-fencible recruit "a nondescript half-sailor, half-soldier, as efficient as neither." To take the most optimistic view, the Volunteer Corps has improved morale for ordinary citizens, giving them a purpose other than to sit by the window and wring their hands at the specter of French legions marching up the High Road.

We are, of course, nervous about what the outbreak of war will mean for all of you in the West Indies. The *Almanack* predicts that "the Genius of the British Nation would triumph over all its adverse Fortune," but we are more assured by the knowledge that Commodore Hood's fleet preceded you by several months. Frank said that the one thing the government did properly was to begin calling up 50,000 seamen at the beginning of the year. It cannot provide satisfaction to any supporter of liberty that press gangs are needed to meet the quota, yet one cannot see any other choice. Because Army and Militia units were severely depleted during the "peace," only the Royal Navy stands as a "wooden wall" between us and the Corsican.

Sincerely,
J. Austen

———

19 July1803

Dear Miss Austen

I am pleased to hear that Henry and Eliza are safe. I shared your sensible worries and tried to dissuade Eliza from her plans. They did not want to understand that the outbreak of peace, being inadvertent, was not likely to hold. My help in their cause was overstated. A person engaged in commerce develops contacts with a certain category of tradesmen who have exceedingly informal relationships with authorities on both sides of the Channel. These enterprising sailors prove adept at moving cargo when normal shipping is interrupted. (Would you believe that it is the Dennis looms that provide Josephine her fine cotton stockings?) I did nothing more than deliver your family the name of a captain or two in case of duress. It was up to Eliza to charm their way through the French checkpoints and onto a boat and safely home.

You'll be pleased to know that Dr. Herschel, who also traveled to France during the peace, returned safely. His most onerous task was listening to Buonaparte expound upon science while puttering about his flower beds; the doctor's reward was to be fed fruit-flavored ice cream.

I agree with your general observations of Mr. Davy. Unlike many natural philosophers, he is as much at home on the stage as in the laboratory.

Dr. Herschel and I attended several of his lectures. Davy speaks of chemistry as a poet speaks of a woman's beauty. (I recognized at least one poet in the audience at one presentation, Mr. Coleridge? Looking for inspiration and metaphor, I should think.) Davy's genius is unquestioned. Whether it manifests itself more in discovery or in promotion of his enthusiasms, remains to be seen.

I cannot speak of a First Cause. I do believe that Man will eventually come to understand most of the "minute and complex sequences" now hidden in Nature's bosom. The world will be a better place when we do. I agree that no amount of understanding will ever unravel the mystery behind the world. Davy and others believe that our knowledge is increasing so rapidly that within a few decades we will know all of Nature that can be known. I suspect the opposite. I rather believe our efforts are like the peeling of an onion. Understanding one layer will open yet another new layer beneath. And the universe is a very large onion indeed. Davy's personification of the world is appropriate in one sense. Like a woman, Nature will always surprise.

Sincerely,
A. Dennis
HMS Centaur
North American Station

———⁘⁘⁘⁘———

11 September 1803

Dear Mr. Dennis

Despite my diligent perusal of the newspapers and gazettes, I have been unable, since my last letter, to uncover anything of significance in the greater world of business or science. Perhaps the imminent arrival of autumn brings the fallow season for great enterprises. I do have news, which I hesitate to mention because of its miniature *nature, if you will. It may not hold much interest for you, and I do not wish to come across as being overly forward or proud for what might strike you as a minor accomplishment—if anything at all. Yet I am proud—there, I admit it.*

I have but one talent beyond those of the ordinary lady, and that is to write. Perhaps it is better to say that I have no interest beyond the ordinary lady except to write, for until now, despite having produced two other novels,

I have remained unpublished. Having thus foreshadowed my point, I have no choice, I suppose, except to merely state it: I have sold a book. It is called Susan, *and it has been taken by Richard Crosbie & Co., of Stationers' Hall Court. I shall be a published novelist! Henry arranged for the sale. The price paid was only ten pounds, but* Susan *has been stipulated for early publication. Mr. Crosbie even includes the novel in* Flowers of Literature, *his preview of books for 1804.*

Modest as the price may be, Susan *is a start. Henry is very enthusiastic, believing that its publication will lead to my other books coming into print. I am fortunate that my father encouraged me to become a writer, for there is little else that a woman of my station can do to provide for herself. Uncertain as I am of success, the plan is to attribute the book to "A Lady," so that I may avoid unnecessary embarrassment if the only purchasers are members of my family.*

Sincerely,
J. Austen

———◦◦◦———

28 October 1803

Dear Miss Austen

I must begin with two contradictory statements. The first is that I have no liking at all for novels. I have never understood the idea of reading about the imagined lives of others when there is so much actual living to be done for ourselves. The second is that I have nothing but admiration for your having completed not one—but three!—creative works of book length.

I read a good deal on subjects that interest me. I am sorry to say that these topics do not include fiction. I have not read a literary book since university. I do not know whether the fault lies in what my sisters read—I have occasionally picked up one of their novels but have seldom gone beyond a page—or in my temperament. I do not wish to try to master the fantastic when I struggle so hard to master life itself.

Yet I appreciate the skill and dedication that must be required in writing a long and complicated work. I can barely compose a letter. The written word comes as hard for me as the spoken. After reading one of your letters, I feel as I might at a ball, trying to match your graceful footwork with my farmer's stomp. I work tirelessly to compose a response that you will not look down upon. You cannot hear my stutter in a letter. But I struggle just as hard to form the words. What might take you two hours to write takes me two days. I call upon the officers on the ship—anyone who is the least bit literate—to help with what I have to say. What you write, I manufacture.

To think that you have spent—what, a year, more?—to compose a work on a single topic, about a set of characters, is beyond my ken. I salute you, madam! I look forward to seeing your book. If only to gauge the intellectual effort it must have entailed.

I would be pleased to hear more of your efforts. It would be interesting to understand how a serious person approaches a creative endeavor over a long period of time. As opposed to how the rest of the world approaches ordinary work—the kind I do.

We have had matters of significance unfold here. War preparations have begun with an indolence typical of the Islands. We are formally blockading Santo Domingo. It is a success because no French ships have yet arrived to test it. Even with Hood's fleet at our disposal, the holdings of the French are dispersed enough—positioned smartly enough—to make decisive action unlikely. To ensure victory, one would need to mass all of one's forces, leaving one's own holdings unattended and open to surprise attack. Few commanders have such nerve. And we British must also constantly look over our shoulders at the Spanish. They are friends when we move on the French. They are enemies when we venture too close to their ports. They are thieves when we leave our belongings unprotected. Spanish policy is to be friends with whichever side they think will win.

So ships circle. Each side waits for the other side to make a mistake. It is a dance that even you might admire.

This military acumen comes from Lieutenant Maurice, whom I recently met when I became informally attached to the Centaur, *Commodore Hood's flagship. I have been passed around like a poor relation. The result, however, is that I have already seen more of the Caribbean than a typical sailor. Please send Dr. Herschel a note to expect several shipments of mine. They were got off before the restrictions imposed by the new hostilities.*

If things get hot, I am threatened to be dropped off on a shoal with my equipment until the engagement is over. Lieutenant Maurice's jocularity on this topic is now taken up by the crew whenever a strange sail appears on the horizon. I do not seek war, as do some young men. Though I confess some fascination with the prospect. My main task in battle, if one should arise, is to remain out of the way. Most of this crew has seen action. They seem of a sober disposition. Neither the officers nor the sailors appear to harbor the kind of rashness that would blunder us into danger.

Sincerely,
A. Dennis
HMS Centaur
North American Station

———⟋⟍⟋⟍⟋⟍———

23 December 1803

Dear Mr. Dennis

Your life on the North American Station and mine in England are similar in one regard. I, too, have been passed around like a poor relation. Except that we are not so much like poor relations as we are poor relations. Cassandra and I have been to Charmouth, Uplyme, Pinny, Godmersham, Ashe, Bath, Lyme Regis, and now Bath again. The most exciting event of all these excursions was also the most frightening. A large fire broke out near our quarters in Lyme Regis. Though we were never directly threatened, we were alarmed; for there is nothing more frightening than a large, out-of-control fire that is so close one can feel the heat on one's skin. It took a number of hours for peace to be restored.

My father and mother joined me on the visit to Godmersham to see brother Edward. Like traveling minstrels, we earn our victuals by entertaining our hosts and helping with the odd family task. One afternoon chasing the children around, two witty rejoinders, and three darned stockings will earn a meal, by my estimation. I hope you have as much success entertaining your naval colleagues when they are not making you stand in the corner during battle.

We have lovely quarters in Bath, but I must declare that I enjoy being on the road more than at home. Though much of the city is new, it seems as old and tired as my aunt and uncle. Indeed, they are typical of its inhabitants. One hears ceaselessly about its glory days, not so very many years ago. People of the highest quality once came to Bath to escape the noise and bustle of London. Today, it is not people of the highest quality who come here but rather those who hope to find the people of the highest quality. Instead, they find only others like themselves—those who lack the ability, the personality, or the financial wherewithal to succeed somewhere else. Bath has become a town whose population aspires to attach themselves to someone better.

I fear that my own family may somewhat fit this description. We did not come here expressly for such purposes, perhaps. Bath was a town of much joy to my parents when they were young—they married here. Like most children, I suspect, I think of my mother and father in terms of their parental roles. Except for the manner in which my father still dotes upon my mother, I have no sense of them at all as a young romantic couple. I assume that Steventon is where their hearts lie because that is where all their children were born and where we were raised in a very happy life. It is a lesson in humility to recognize that they returned to Bath in the hope of re-creating the pleasure of their courtship days—from that time before children and responsibilities.

Once I understood this impetus, I was pleased for them and regretted the disinclination with which I greeted their desire to return to Bath. (I registered my protest by fainting dead away.) I am certain, too, that they hoped that Cassandra and I would feel, or perhaps discover, the same happiness in the social circle here that they once knew. Yet we find only a desperate effort to seek amusement by people who are themselves not very amusing. Almost every day I return home feeling that never have so many words been exchanged in the course of so little good conversation. I suspect that you saw enough of Bath to know that it no longer has either the charm of the Country or the liveliness of the Town.

Still, we stay busy with parents and a few good friends. We escort our much loved uncle to the waters almost every day, and we shepherd our demanding aunt from shop to shop with a careful eye that she does not slip an item of fashion into her pocket before she has remembered to pay for it. Not too long ago, a neighbor's flower pot found its way onto her doorstep. Like Macbeth we wonder, "Who can bid the tree unfix his earth-bound root?" Perhaps your studies will lead you to discover exotic plants that are capable of pulling themselves up out of the ground, walking half a block, and settling down again like a roosting chicken.

You know what January is like in England. Rain, wind, a flurry of snow just when it looks as though it will clear. We would none of us object to a few days in Barbados. A rainy day lasts longer in Bath than a rainy week in Hampshire. A walk in the rain in Steventon has a kind of charm; the lightly falling rain patters out a kind of lullaby. I would come home happy—and feeling the need of a nap! A walk in soggy Bath leaves me gloomy. The rain does not refresh but seems to leach something out of me.

I return home feeling that I have the city's tears upon my cloak. I cannot explain why this should be. It is in the afternoons, when my work is done, that I sometimes drift into melancholy.

I should not make too much of this sensation. A bracing dish of hot tea and some time with Cass will snap me out of the bleakness. And of course we look forward to the balls and other events to attend, with all the hurry and amusement they bring. Even with it being out of season, we keep as lively as we can. Fewer crowds and visitors, but sometimes a cozier and friendlier atmosphere. Everyone at the assembly rooms, I must report, wants to know when you and Alethea will return. Many a young lady sighs when she hears that you are off at sea. I may have led a few to believe that you have taken up the life of a whaling captain.

We hope to travel again when the season improves. Despite the usual concerns of traveling weather, leaky luggage, and dirty roads, I do enjoy the change of scenery. We are so much in the habit of mobility that we are able to get off in a matter of hours. Though experience teaches us to pack lightly, we sometimes find ourselves with companions who carry as much equipage as any natural philosopher on a year-long journey to the other side of the world. Such travelers invariably complain when the burden is too great for the horses. These people are not able to make the connection between the weight of their belongings and the requirement that they get out of the coach and drag themselves through mud on foot.

Nor do they consider the inconvenience it causes their fellow passengers who limit themselves to one trunk of reasonable size. I imagine that during the great migrations of the past there was always that one couple who brought more than the rest of the village combined, and I imagine that they will continue to plague the traveling public in whatever conveyances are invented in the future.

Our expeditions are not scientific, but as you see we study the unusual creatures on the road with assiduous care.

Be assured that your family and friends keep you in their thoughts and prayers. Be safe, Mr. Dennis.

Sincerely,
J. Austen

Chapter 18

27 November 1803

Jane

We have seen action here. The Commodore determined to break the French with an attack upon Martinique, their most strategic possession. Given the general lassitude of military endeavors on both sides, he hoped to surprise them. Apparently his thinking was too obvious. The French were ready, and they sent many of our brave boys to their deaths within the first few minutes. Fortunately, the Commodore recognized his error. He ordered a withdrawal as quickly as possible. We lost marines from the Centaur *in the engagement, as well as other men throughout the fleet.*

Of most anguish to me personally were the serious injuries to Lieutenant Maurice. Our friendship has become congenial over the months. He does not have wide knowledge, but his fine mind absorbs everything he sees and hears. The poor fellow was seriously injured when a magazine exploded. I had not been left on a shoal but rather in a relatively safe position with the landing boats during our advance. It was my duty to help bring Lieutenant Maurice and several other wounded men to safety. This was an experience almost impossible to recount. They are in bloody and terrible pain, suffering insults to the flesh that no human should have to bear, and they are thanking me *for providing aid. I did nothing more than what one would do in escorting an elderly person across the street. Yet they heaped me with praise and cried at my doing them a service. It was the least I could do for those shattered boys. I felt unworthy that I could not do more.*

When we had them all back on board and attended to by the surgeons, I had to sit down to recover my wits, the experience had been so disorienting. Covered in blood. That it was not mine made my reaction unaccountably worse. How does one respond to the actuality of being drenched in the sacred essence that was once within *another human being?*

Ashton

⸺⸙⸺

17 January 1804

Ashton

You cannot imagine the shudder that occasioned your last letter—to realize that you had been in battle, dealing with all the horrors of war, while I prattled on about dreary old Bath and my excursions to every tourist town in the south of England. How trivial all of my comments must have seemed after you tended to your comrade and the other injured men. I cannot tell you how proud I am that you are helping the Royal Navy in their efforts to thwart Buonaparte and drive the French from the Caribbean. I wrote immediately to both my brothers to let them know how even a gentleman and civilian from Hampshire is willing to assist when the situation requires. Because you are not a soldier, and did not enlist for this war, I feel more worry for you than I do for Charles and Frank, who have had years of training and are inured to the sacrifices required by the sea. Do be cautious. Do not let your innate patriotism lead you to the kind of foolish courage that results in sad notices in the newspapers.

Your friend,
Jane

⸺⸙⸺

15 April 1804

Dear Miss Austen

Even a letter that drips with sadness—to build upon your own imagery in your letter of December—is of welcome comfort after the months we have experienced on the Centaur. It brings home, home—if I make sense.

I must apologize for the brusque and emotional nature of my last letter. My head was in an uproar. I dashed off the spinning thoughts without any

122

*regard for how my words might affect you on the other end. I did not mean
to shock you or offend your feelings.*

*Things are much improved here since last I wrote. Especially with
Lieutenant Maurice. To give you an idea of his redoubtable nature,
only six weeks after his injuries he led another landing party, this one
to Diamond Rock, an island just off Martinique. It dominates the
approaches to the main ports. We took ashore a number of men and
hauled guns up the sheer sides of a cliff wall to the top of the rock. My
size for once proved to be of value. We needed every last ounce of strength
from every man jack of us—every windlass, every block and tackle, every
inch of cordage on the ship—to lift the heavy guns several hundred feet
straight up. It was worth the week of hot, sweaty labor. We approached
on the side away from the main island—the French could not see and
intervene. If they had come upon us, we would have been in great trouble.
During the operation, the* Centaur *was lashed to the island as tightly as
a woman's corset.*

*Because of the wind and currents, the only safe way to cross between
the northern isle of Martinique and the southern isle of St. Lucia is to
pass in front of Diamond Rock. Only now the way is no longer safe. The
angle is so severe that we can fire down on the French but they can barely
elevate their guns enough to fire on us. By owning the high ground, our
cannons chase ships far out to sea. They cannot beat their way back against
the winds and currents. Lieutenant Maurice was not merely in charge of
the operation—it was his idea. It was one of those notions that is beyond
ridiculous until it succeeds. I asked him whether he took special delight in
pounding the French supply ships because Martinique was the source of his
injuries and pain. He responded with an enigmatic smile. Defeating the
French is all the satisfaction he requires.*

*Since our shot has begun to rain down upon them, the French have
made several sallies to try to clear us off. We turn them away before they
get within a quarter of a mile. Our fort is virtually impregnable. The
French would have to set their entire fleet against us. Even so, if we had
more guns, we could sink half the ships before they could overwhelm us.
I say "us" because the Lieutenant has given me a few auxiliary duties.
My help in hoisting the guns ensured my acceptance by the crew. I now
assist the surgeon, though since the original battle there have been only a
few fevers and minor injuries. Because we lack enough officers, I also have*

the unofficial responsibility of mustering one of the squads to their position during an attack.

Being the only person on board with an agricultural background, I have also been assigned a small herd of goats and some chickens and guinea hens. These supplement our scanty fare. I am the steward, the Mr. Fletcher of Diamond Rock, albeit one far less skilled in the duties of the particular station. Lieutenant Maurice takes a droll pleasure in assigning me tasks beneath my status. I am not offended. In the event that things get hot again, he must know whether he can count on me. And the crew must also know whether I am to be an aid or an encumbrance to them. My taking on a few tedious tasks will not give them a clear answer, of course. When the battle rages I might well be using the goats as a shield; at least they know I will not be expecting tea to be served while the shot is flying.

Fort is not actually the correct word, I must hasten to add. Maurice's other brilliant idea was to request that we be commissioned. "We are fully at sea, and we have already won several battles with the French," he told Hood by way of rationale. "I guarantee that no number of enemy sail will ever cause this vessel to flee." The Commodore practically split himself open laughing. But he did not hesitate to grant the request. The decision greatly raised spirits among the men, who are facing many months of service upon a hot, dry rock. I now stand proudly (when I am not writing, where I make a boulder as a table) upon HMS Diamond Rock, a sloop in the Royal Navy. Among other benefits, I suffer a good deal less seasickness upon this sloop than on any other ship. Lieutenant Maurice was also made a captain. At least, everyone now calls him Captain. I believe he is a Captain on Diamond Rock and a Lieutenant when he is back aboard the Commodore's ship. You will have to ask your brothers to explain the rules.

I know that the Royal Navy is the domain of the Austen family. I hope my informal deputation with this vessel does not represent a usurpation of your family privilege. Diamond Rock, of course, could not hope to keep up with any ship captained by an Austen.

Yet I sign my location with no little pride.

Sincerely,
A. Dennis
HMS Diamond Rock
North American Station

3 June 1804

Dear Mr. Dennis

Please do not worry about anything you may write to me regarding your experiences, in the Caribbean or elsewhere. I understood immediately that you were writing from your heart about an episode that would trouble any man of feeling. Indeed, you showed more sensitivity in those few lines than in all the years that I have known you. I do not mean to criticize your past behavior; rather, the experience must have truly been heart-rending for it to break through the reserve that British gentlemen work so hard to maintain. It was honestly refreshing, to speak the truth. I recognize that I am a convenient correspondent, for you could not have written such thoughts to a man, because doing so would have broken the masculine code. Nor could you have written to your sisters, for fear of the alarm and upset your letter would have brought to Hants House. Your mother already swoons to every market gyration. Who knows what such a missive might have occasioned.

If a letter to me helps you deal with exigencies that none of us away from war can truly understand, and can lessen consternation elsewhere in your life, please do not hesitate to pick up a pen. I keep everything you write, close.

I heard nothing but commendation from my brothers regarding your assistance in the assault upon Martinique, and they shared your appreciation of the Lieutenant's sound thinking and good humor in launching the Diamond Rock. *Frank remains on patrol in the Channel. Charles expects to be posted to the West Indies at any time. I told him you will be much easier to find than he might have expected, as you are not likely to drag anchor during heavy seas.*

As penance for the domestic chatter of my previous letter, I shall bring you up to date on the latest political and scientific marvels.

The first is that an anti-slavery bill has passed the House of Commons. It will never pass the House of Lords, of course, but Mr. Wilberforce has finally achieved something. I do not know whether we should admire his persistence or should feel embarrassment for his foolhardiness. I do not claim to have any knowledge or understanding of Africans—I have seen only one or two in London, and I assume that they were free. I think back to Cowper's poem:

> *"Slaves cannot breathe in England; if their lungs*
> *Receive our air, that moment they are free;*
> *They touch our country, and their shackles fall."*

I do not like the idea of any peoples being in chains, but I do not understand how one man has the audacity to tell half the world how they should behave. And to speak the truth, I do not have much patience for the few abolitionists I have met in society. Their attention to the issue seems to be based on fashion—and proof that they are holier—rather than on a sense of humanity. I am too harsh, I know, for slavery is a terrible thing; but I do not accept pretension as a moral force.

Other news comes from France, where the Senate has voted to make Buonaparte emperor. I doubt that they felt they had much of an option in the matter. Not precisely in response, but perhaps more necessary because of his accretion of more power, our Corps of Volunteers has grown to more than three hundred and eighty thousand men. This strength should give Buonaparte concern that we will knock his new crown off his head if he were to undertake the invasion he constantly threatens.

You may have heard of the other French matter, because you are far closer to the object, which is that Buonaparte has sold the Louisiana Territory to the Americans for 15 million dollars. According to the published accounts, the land involved is everything from the Mississippi River to a mountain range far to the west. The purchase, at pennies an acre, doubles the size of the colonies. I doubt this expansion will make it easier for us to ever recover them. Perhaps when we are done with France!

On a happier note, perhaps, I will tell you of important medical news that has all the ladies in a buzz. A depilatory has been patented, promising "beautifully smooth skin." The price is only one pound, including post. Among my acquaintances, those who will gladly pay are not necessarily the ones who would benefit the most. ... Every week in the newspaper one sees more and more in the way of cosmetics that offer science in support of their claims. Is civilization advancing that rapidly in support of the beautification of women, or are commercial interests becoming ever more creative in their efforts to sell?

Speaking of commercial interests, Portsmouth has become as full of merchant vessels as Covent Garden is of carriages and sedan chairs. (I paraphrase my brother, from another context.) The merchant fleet dashed to safety as soon as war recommenced, and ventures out now only when a man-of-war is available for convoy duty. As I am sure she has told you, Alethea *relates that the Dennis ships are as aggressive as possible in setting forth on their voyages. So far, she says, business has not been seriously restricted.*

On a more scientific note, I will tell you what I have read about the latest technical marvel. This one does not entail facial creams or even the subtle mixtures and strange gases being investigated by Mr. Davy, but rather iron and steel and great puffing engines. I suspect this will appeal to you rather more than chemistry. A mining engineer by the name of Richard Trevithick has created a steam engine on wheels that he claims will revolutionize transportation. This "loco-motive," as they call the mechanism, is able to propel itself upon two parallel rails—of wood or iron, I am not sure which. In its first test, the engine carried ten tons of iron and seventy passengers nine miles along a tramway in Wales. It took less than five hours! Even I can recognize that this is an astonishing performance. I do not know whether, as Mr. Trevithick claims, it will become practical to run rails between cities and carry passengers and freight all over the country. However, to someone who has to drag her skirts through miles of muddy roads every time it rains, the prospect of sitting in a carriage riding upon a solid foundation has a certain appeal. What do you think—shall we build a "rail-way" from Hants House to London?

Fondly,
J. Austen

———

29 July 1804

Dear Miss Austen

I had never thought about slavery until I came to the West Indies. Here, British gentry enjoy their drinks on the veranda while being fanned by their house slaves, and they complain about the laziness of their field slaves. But is it any better in England? Hang a starving man—banish him to Australia—for stealing a loaf of bread! French slaves here hate their masters so much that they provide us food and tell us what they have overheard about French plans.

I very much appreciate your information on locomotives. There are many steam engines in operation these days. To pull water out of mine shafts. This is likely how Mr. Trevithick became involved. But mining engines lack the power to move themselves. Never mind to pull a load of the size that you describe. High-pressure systems may possess the power, but they have the unfortunate habit of exploding. I look forward to learning how he has overcome this problem.

We have, indeed, heard of the Louisiana Purchase. It will benefit England because it takes New Orleans out of the hands of the French and removes France as a power anywhere in North America. The understanding here—according to Captain Maurice—is that the Americans would have soon taken the city. It is too important to be left in the hands of a foreign power. Buonaparte was wise to sell before his prize was stolen.

France has already withdrawn from San Domingo because of the slave revolt and the loss of so many of her troops to fever. (Things are not much better for us. Our surgeon, Dr. Uglow, said that half of the ninety thousand soldiers and sailors so far stationed in the West Indies have died of what he calls "that ardent and merciless destroyer, the yellow fever.") San Domingo's sugar, coffee, and tobacco provided most of France's colonial profits. If we can dislodge the French from their few remaining possessions in the Caribe, they will be totally removed from the New World.

However, what Buonaparte loses on one side of the Atlantic he will seek to recoup on the other. Have no doubt that the 15 million dollars will be put to use in the war against us. You may not know that it was British bankers who brokered the transaction between the United States and France—a deal that could finance the invasion of their own country!

I realize that we are halfway through the year and you have said no more about your novel. Did Susan have her come-out? Has "A Lady" replaced Mrs. Radcliffe as England's leading authoress? You never described to me how you go about your work.

Sincerely,
A. Dennis
HMS Diamond Rock
North American Station

———∽∾⋘⋙∾∽———

21 Sept. 1804

Dear Mr. Dennis

I have not provided any news about Susan because there is no news to report. Notwithstanding the stipulation for early release, it has not yet been published. Henry's inquiries have brought only equivocation. Your reference to Mrs. Radcliffe struck close to home, as it may be that she is the reason for the delay. Many of Mr. Crosbie's stable of books are of the Gothic variety, and Henry fears that the publisher may be worried about the effect of my novel on his overall sales, for Susan *turns the Gothic novel upside down.* Susan *regards a young woman—"in training for a heroine"—who creates a great deal of trouble for herself by believing she lives within a Gothic novel. I would like to think that delays are part and parcel of the book business rather than that Mr. Crosbie is rethinking publication. We remain hopeful, though not perhaps confident, for publication later this year.*

Being unlike any book before, Susan *may find a niche or oblivion. I cannot help it. I have no desire to repeat the usual ladies' novels of the day. I believe it is worthy of publication, but I have an invincible distrust of my own judgment about these things. I have no way of knowing whether its sitting-room topics will interest you, but* Susan *is set in Bath, so even if you do not find the writing to your taste, you might enjoy the setting.*

As for the nature of authorship itself, I do not believe it differs from any other kind of work. It is like a large, complex weaving project, except that the designs are mental rather than physical. One must create and maintain threads throughout the entire artifice, creating an interesting design. There are times when—like managing your accounts—the effort is tedious. Too often I am not at all in a humor for writing; I must write on till I am. There are times when one is so stymied by the question of "what happens next" that one wishes to throw the whole thing in the fire. And there are times when the work is exhilarating. Many of my best ideas come when I have abandoned writing for the day and take up actual needlework. Sometimes a great line occurs to me and I laugh out loud and rush over to the writing table to jot down the words before I forget.

One value of doing intellectual rather than physical labor is that it is much easier—though still quite frustrating—to revise words than to unwind and restart "real" projects. On the other hand, it is almost impossible to see minor mistakes in a shawl, and even a flawed shawl can keep one warm in the winter. Other artwork, painting and sculpture, can be enjoyed half-finished. Yet fiction must be complete and perfect or it does not exist at all. A novel is like a building, both in the nature and complexity of its construction and the fact that it must be watertight—from foundation to roof—before it is of any use at all. Though, in truth, I do not build edifices. I build intricate dollhouses.

I have revised my books several times, and after each revision I have put the novel away quite satisfied. Yet when I return to the work a few months later, I find that it is full of unnatural conduct and forced difficulties, or that the behavior of a character is wholly inconsistent with what has come before, or that I have used an unsupportable coincidence—I wince at terrible dialogue—I strike with mortification one of those lines I thought was brilliant. Can you imagine an architect spending a lifetime redesigning a single building? That is sometimes how I feel. And of course the author is more than the architect: She must also serve as carpenter, painter, and all-around drudge. Each redesign requires the ripping out of floorboards and the knocking down of walls; then everything must be rebuilt, replastered, and whitewashed. I never know whether to be glad that I have standards to which I aspire or sad that my writing falls so far below where I wish it to be. But I muddle on. An artist cannot do anything slovenly. Sisyphus was too clever for his own good; he must have been a writer.

There are a few women of my acquaintance who are also writers, yet I have never been able to approach them. Embarrassment in the company of those who have seen success; superiority, I fear, toward those whose conversation makes me believe they will not produce anything worthwhile. Thus I have no idea whether my insecurity—my dissatisfaction with what I produce—is personal to me or endemic to the authorial trade. Do you suppose our great playwrights ever felt uncertainty about their works? Of course, Shakespeare could tell by the audience's reaction whether or not a scene played as he intended, and he could revise it before the next production!

Much as I enjoy travel, our constant movement makes it difficult to write on a regular basis. I find it necessary to have a quiet, regular time and place to create anything worth keeping. And it has been frankly difficult to be diligent toward my craft when no one outside my family wishes to read what I have done. How much more enthusiasm I brought to my writing table when I thought I was soon to be published!

Sincerely,
J. Austen

4 November 1804

Dear Mr. Dennis

   Two such interesting things have happened that I felt the necessity to write to you before hearing your response to my last letter. Cassandra and I have been on the march again. One expedition took us to the east to see Alethea, who has in the last half year or so been able to open the doors of Hants House to us without any remonstrance from your dear mother. It is with some satisfaction that Mrs. Dennis accepts our greetings when we pass in the hall. Our attendance in the role as her daughters' friends is a positive juxtaposition to the role it could have been. ... On this latest visit she took part in the exchange of local news when we sat at table. The more time that passes, the more she seems desirous of treating the events of December 1802 as being the kind of misunderstanding that any longstanding friendship might on occasion have to overcome.

   I am under the impression that she has made a deliberate decision to treat the matter as a misunderstanding in order for it to come to pass in exactly that way. I mean that she changed her mind, which directed a change in her feelings, rather than the other way around; for I doubt that her feelings ever would have altered. I thank her for this display of mental fortitude, as it has enabled Cass and me to see dear Alethea personally.

   I cannot help but compare the manner in which Mr. Ashton Dennis and Miss Alethea Dennis shoulder the affairs of their family. I remember seeing you in the library, surrounded by business correspondence and invoices, which you set upon as a terrier sets upon a rat. Alethea resembles more an heiress from the country in her first shopping expedition up to London. She races from one set of problems to another as if she cannot wait to open the next box to see what delightful new hat or dress awaits her. You correctly foresaw that she would complain in exacting detail about the way in which Little Brother left her to puzzle out on her own some subtlety of supply or demand; yet the very nature of her grievances implies the mastery of a subject with many intricacies. I would label this behavior "boasting by complaint" except that her joy in the work is so obvious and so well earned that I do not wish to sound approbative. One reason your mother frets so is that she fears her daughter is not up to the task, being a female, or does not take the responsibility seriously. Nothing could be further from the truth. If she exudes the giddiness of a young girl unable to decide between French and Viennese lace, it is because a woman has no other means by which to display her satisfaction in the management of a financial empire. And

Alethea is careful to repeat the refrain that the world insists upon, that she does nothing more than execute the instructions she receives from her brother.

Do not doubt that she exhibits her own kind of ferocity, Mr. Dennis. Indeed, I hope you have considered how you will extract the management of your enterprises from her upon your return. Though she will graciously accede to your wishes, she will also make herself indispensable in the many obligations you find so burdensome.

Let me relate the most interesting encounter of our current stay in Lyme, which is one of our favorite seaside towns—the main street seems to be almost hurrying into the water. We always visit the shops and walk upon The Cobb when we are at Lyme. Naturally, we see acquaintances from our regular visits. I also met a new friend, Miss Anderson, who is pleasant enough to walk with. There is a place on the edge of town, near the coach stop at the inn, where one finds the tables at which locals sell fruits and vegetables—all the usual market things—as well as items laid out for the visitors. As we walked by one small stand, a high little voice sang out, "Would you like a fossil? They fall from the sky!"

Unless I am seeking a particular gift, I avoid the hawkers at all cost. The moment one responds, there is an obligation to purchase something. It is as if they are being paid for their time rather than for their wares. But in this case I could not resist the angelic voice, which (I quickly learned) belonged to a girl by the name of Mary. She could not have been more than five years old. She had brown hair, unremarkable features, and the untidiness of a child who spends more time out of doors than in. (This I see as a good untidiness!) Yet it was not only her voice that was angelic but her smile. Together, they could not but focus my attention on her. "They do not actually fall from the sky," she said. "They fall from the cliffs after a heavy rain. Or rather, Father digs them out."

At this point we were introduced to her father, Mr. Anning, whom I recognized as a cabinet maker who recently provided an estimate for us involving a repair. He seemed a little embarrassed at the salesmanship of his little girl. Though by his speech and bearing he is a man of little education, he takes his fossil collecting seriously. He explained to us where on the cliffs the best fossils are found and how he protects them from damage as he extracts them from the rocks. Selling "tourist fossils," he explained, helped pay for his work; but he has larger specimens that he considers highly valuable.

"They are a million years old!" Mary chimed in.

"But the stars are a million years old," I said. "The fossils must be younger than that."

"No," she said, and turned toward the cliffs with an expression as serious as that of any professionals I have ever seen embarking upon the subject in which they are versed. "Look how high the cliff is. Look at the number of layers. It's the biggest cake in the world."

"It is how I explain fossils to the children," Mr. Anning explained. "So they know that what we do is important. ... And, of course, that things are very old."

(Perhaps you should see if your colleagues in London might be interested in Mr. Anning's work. I have mentioned it to Miss Herschel in the hope that she or her brother may do them a service as well. Speaking of the Herschels, I relay the following message from the doctor by means of his sister: "We have news that Mr. Alexander von Humboldt returned from South America with 60,000 specimens. Mr. Dennis is short approximately 58,500. Encourage him to exert himself.")

But to return to my story. By now, of course, the Anning family had earned a purchase. I asked Mary to pick out a fossil for me that lay within my modest science budget, a fossil that she thought I would particularly enjoy.

She brought back a shell, one that was very small (in proportion to its price) but well formed and in pristine condition. She wrapped the fossil in a tiny bit of cloth and handed it to me as if it were a diamond.

"It is old," she said.

Her soul, shining through those dark eyes, was as ancient as any of the creatures laid out upon her table.

Sincerely,
J. Austen

———————————

31 December 1804

To My Dear Correspondent of Convenience

We have had delays in the receipt of provisions and letters—the result of the capture of the Fort Diamond, *our escort. I had not mentioned to you that we had a vessel assigned to us, making it handy to harass smaller enemy vessels nearby and to provide easy resupply. While the* Fort

Diamond was off gathering water and food, it managed to get seized by the French. The crew was asleep below, the commander too busy fishing off the stern to notice the enemy approaching silently from the bow. The ship was taken before the crew could rouse themselves from slumber. For all of the sacrifice, hardship, and bloodshed that this war has brought upon sailors and soldiers around the world, I cannot tell you of the fury the capture of the ship has caused here. Not from a battle or a storm—but from foolhardiness out of an Italian comedy! The loss of Fort Diamond *has severely limited our operations.*

This has been the only French victory. They continue to come at Diamond Rock. *They approach to a certain distance, we blow a boat or two out of the water, and they retreat. We repeat the performance every several weeks. I would call the situation another comedy except that on almost every occasion a few French soldiers die. "Vanquishing the foe" is a ringing phrase, and it is good to have any victory, but one feels no exultation to see bodies floating on the tide. There is only the relief that they are not the bodies of one's friends.*

As much as I admire the courage of these men who come against us at an impossible disadvantage, Lieutenant Maurice condemns the stupidity of the superiors who send them out like clockwork to be blown to pieces. Until the loss of our tender, we too made raids upon the enemy. But the lieutenant always calculates carefully. He makes sure we have the advantage of surprise or numbers. He makes sure our men have a way out if things go badly. He never risks the men's lives foolishly. He is bold in his strategy, cautious in his execution. I know nothing of the business of war, except that his style of leadership makes the men revere him. Recognizing that he does all he can to protect them, they fight all the harder on his behalf. That, of course, increases our chances of winning, even when the odds are not the best. Compare his approach to that of the French commander. Sends his men into harm's way hoping for a miracle. I fear that this is the approach of too many leaders in their quest for riches and glory.

Your comments on the Anning family are a reminder that I have given up my aspirations to be a natural philosopher. Even before we settled here, I had relegated specimen collecting and preservation to volunteers from the crew. They rather enjoyed the work—change of pace from swabbing decks and repairing sails. I prefer to kill only those animals that are dangerous, that are vermin, or that I plan to consume. In the first category, we have killed a few of the dangerous snakes known as fer-de-lance. We have also taken quite a lot of a plant called the callaloo. Tastes like sour spinach but protects against scurvy. Samples of both of those have been preserved. Otherwise, it strikes me as unnatural to kill creatures only to study them. And I cannot abide the task of preserving them. I would rather eat sand. I love to learn about the natural world. But direct study is too slow and arduous. I suppose the world is a much more orderly place because geology moves at a leisurely pace. One would not be happy if the British Isles were to rise and fall in the sea every week. But I need a science that moves more at the pace of a fox hunt. Something we can chase today, not accumulate data upon for years and decades. I must leave the work to more patient fellows. Please do not tell my fellow natural philosophers—they would shun me.

Ah—but listen to little Miss Mary.

Sincerely,
A. Dennis
HMS Diamond Rock
North American Station

Chapter 19

19 December 1804

Dear Mr. Dennis

I am so weighed down by sadness that I do not have the strength to face the reason directly. I must struggle on and hope that, step by step, I will find the courage to explain what has happened. I must surprise the thought before it crushes me. You will understand, I pray, if you bear with me.

Until I became an adult, Christmas always seemed to me to be the happiest time of the year. The celebration of our Savior's birth, the gathering of family and friends, the balls and parties—the weather must have been dreary to keep the high spirits from getting completely out of hand! And of course my birthday added a personal joy. It was just far enough in advance of Christmas to make it special, yet still close enough to be imbued with the general holiday spirit.

For the last several years, Christmas has not spread joy as it should, and I begin to fear that the time surrounding my birthday is cursed. In the first part of the month, my father's health began to suffer; and this caused my mother to unload her usual cupboard of complaints. As the wife, she must follow the husband's lead in so many ways, but she is determined that she will be the forerunner in the category of ailments. Their illnesses, and the need for everyone to stay indoors, made the first weeks of December very dreary.

Then, today, I heard in a letter from my brother James that Mrs. Lefroy has died as the result of a fall from her horse. Mrs. Lefroy, my Beloved Friend, was killed—on my birthday! Angelic woman, past my power to praise! A friend and ornament of humankind. Dead.

James had seen her in the village and exchanged greetings shortly before the accident and of course was dumbfounded to learn, only a few hours later, that she had been thrown down and struck her head. He recalled her remark that the horse was lazy and stupid. The accident occurred where Overton Road joins with the lane from Polehampton. On more than one long ramble I have stopped at that very spot to rest!

For some reason, the coupling of "my" date with her death doubles the pain. She was my guide and advisor, and I her protégé, for all of my youth. How I will miss her genius, taste, and tenderness of soul. It was her "inexpressible pleasure," she said very kindly, to encourage me. There is no one I admired and respected more—not even my own mother. When I had taken a scolding from my Aunt Perrot or someone else, Mrs. Lefroy would say that what others saw as impetuosity she saw as frank independence, and what others saw as impudence she saw as honest intelligence that would not tolerate deceit or hypocrisy. She added, in her gentle way, that I might exercise more elegance in how I conveyed those qualities. You see how she sought to guide even as she encouraged.

Yet our relationship had become strained—not estranged, because my admiration for her was too deep, but strained—over her nephew Tom, whom you may or may not remember, as I was just twenty years old and you, of course, much younger.

Tom was here years ago for this same holiday season, and he and I were beginning to develop a special friendship when Mrs. Lefroy sent him away. I never heard from or saw Tom again. My father learned years later that he had returned to Ireland, taken up law as planned, and married well. I remained cordial with the family, yet Mrs. Lefroy never offered any explanation for her actions. In fact, she never mentioned Tom's name again—ever. Nor, of course, did I.

Three or four years later, she made a point of introducing me to a young clergyman, also down for Christmas. Mr. Blackall struck me as a piece of noisy perfection, though I was impressed with his immediate recognition that nothing would ever advance between us. If I had never known Tom, perhaps I would have found Mr. Blackall more congenial. But it was almost as if he were a replacement—an exchange, as it were, for young Tom. Every conversation reminded me of who Mr. Blackall was not. For all of her love for me—and I have no doubt that she loved me—it was as if Mrs. Lefroy were offering me a very serviceable second-hand garment in place of the beautiful new pelisse she had snatched away. One cannot swap individuals like clothing!

No one understands better than I that Mrs. Lefroy knew that she could not allow Tom to risk the Langlois inheritance for a young woman lacking a title and a dowry. I was never so naïve not to appreciate the worldly considerations a Lefroy-Austen match would have raised. I let myself be carried away, as any young woman might well have been. But why did she not tell me the plain truth to my face? A younger woman ought to be able to rely on the frankness of a mature and friendly woman. For her to say nothing and then—years later—to offer me a humorless and self-satisfied replacement was more painful than her sending Tom away originally.

My recollections, in the context of her terrible accident, must seem petty. I can see as well as anyone my willfulness in response to her kind offer of an unattached clergyman. (I am not being sarcastic, though I recognize I must sound sarcastic.) But this history encapsulates the grief I feel that we never fully reconciled our differences. She never explained her reasons for sending Tom away, and I never explained my reasons for discouraging Mr. Blackall. She must have felt a lack of gratitude on my part for what she undoubtedly believed was a good turn toward a woman who, by her twenty-fourth birthday, had no real marital prospects. How I now wish I had gone back to Mrs. Lefroy and told her how much regard and affection—deep and genuine love—I felt for her, regardless of what now seems a sad and silly squabble over potential suitors.

I feel terrible at her passing, and even worse that an otherwise perfect friendship could have ever experienced such discord.

I do not wish to end this letter on a sad and self-indulgent note. I know this letter will not reach you in time, but I hope you and your crew had a good Christmas season. Perhaps you were able to get off the Rock for a while?

Sincerely,
J. Austen

---

25 March 1805

Dear Miss Austen

I am sorry to hear of Madam Lefroy's accident and death. Every rider has experienced the sickening sensation of losing control of the horse. Sometimes it is because we become careless and think of the horse as some kind of mechanical conveyance instead of a large, dangerous, and easily frightened animal. Sometimes it is because the horse is startled by something beyond our control. Sometimes it is just bad luck that leads to a stumble when we too are off balance. I have fallen more times than I care to count. I am lucky to have come down safely. I too at times came upon Madam Lefroy on the roads of Hampshire and know her to be an excellent horsewoman. The loss of such a kind and elegant lady is to be regretted.

I know that Alethea will have passed on the condolences from the Dennis family, but please add my commiseration to you and to Madam Lefroy's family.

I recall Tom Lefroy—vaguely—as an intelligent and well-formed young man who attended balls at Hants House. I recall the history of you and Tom in the form of stories that were passed among my sisters. There was no gossip as such—nothing passed outside the family. It was more the clicking of tongues about attentions by the young man that were offered to—withdrawn from—a young lady my family cared about. The Langlois inheritance was discussed among the women, much as men might have discussed business or politics. (I would not have remembered the name of the inheritance except for your letter, only that a large one was at stake.)

I cannot explain to you now the intent of Madam Lefroy in sending Tom off to London. No doubt if your relationship had gone far enough that a proposal was to be expected, Madam Lefroy might have felt answerable to Tom's family in Ireland in a way that could have caused a significant breach. She may have felt that she could not be responsible for a youthful relative in her care risking his inheritance and advancement— regardless of what she felt for you. *She wanted to protect his inheritance. She wanted to protect your heart. Perhaps she let things go further than she should have precisely because, caring for you as she did, she could not bring herself to end it earlier because the relationship brought you joy. Perhaps she let it go because she saw it as a harmless flirtation and did not act until she realized that it had changed into something more serious. That Tom was leading you on when he had no ability to follow through responsibly. It could be that his banishment to London was to save you real humiliation.*

Likewise, I cannot speak to her intentions with the Mr. Blackall. Because he came several years later, I recall him much more clearly. By the time of his arrival I was of an age at which my dislike of him was proportionate to my perception of your attraction to him. I was therefore not displeased at his failure to return to our neighborhood.

Though I have little regard for the historical practice in which the older generation arranges marriage on behalf of young people—often for reasons relating to everything except *the couple's personal happiness—it is also true that many happy, or at least satisfactory, marriages have developed from such arrangements. We might now have a world in which young people more often choose their own mates according to their wishes. But why should we suppose they will do any better in the moment of passion or infatuation than their parents would do in calm reflection? The results of young people choosing for themselves cannot be said to have created more happiness overall. I suspect that half the marriages are more harmonious, the other half more acrimonious.*

Forget for a moment the older generation's legitimate concern with family wealth. Built up over generations or by the hard labor of one generation, it can be so easily wasted by a dissolute son or son-in-law. How many young girls have lost their hearts, and their virtue, by being carried away in an excess of infatuation? How many young men have made promises they are not able to keep, responding to the involuntary needs of their blood rather than to the temperate exercise of their brains?

Again, I do not agree with parents and others deciding for young people. Any adult should be allowed to exercise free will and his—or her—own judgment. But we cannot ignore the dangers of inexperience and naïveté when applied to decisions that have lifelong consequences. "Young love" can be easily confused with the emotionally charged impetuosity that drives most young men and women ... including two whom we shall not identify.

My point—I may not explain it well—is that we all saw you and Madam Lefroy together over the years. Even a self-absorbed youth such as I could see the emotional bond you shared. You were mother and daughter in temperament. Like a mother and daughter, you must have disagreed at some point over a major life decision. If her actions did not work out to your satisfaction, know that she tried to act in your best interest. That is all we can ask of our loved ones. Remember her softly.

A. Dennis
HMS Diamond Rock
North American Station

20 January 1805

Dear Jane and Cass

I have arrived in the West Indies and have taken command of a sloop, the Indian. *It is most rewarding to have my own ship after so many years of service. I am trying to look every bit the captain. Whenever I think I am in over my head, I simply pretend that I am Frank. I put on a sober expression, more frown than smile, and I give the crew something difficult but useful to do.*

One's first ship is always a good ship, but I am pleased with the overall condition of the Indian. *I am learning how the ship handles in different winds and seas, and I am getting my first insights into the strengths and weaknesses of the crew. I have a good first officer and inexperienced but very eager junior officers. The crew is willing to work hard, which speaks well of the previous master.*

I am writing my father too. I know he will be proud. His second son to take command of a ship in the Royal Navy ... and during one of the most important eras in sailing history!

Much to do—

Y *loving brother,*

C. Austen

HMS *Indian*

North American Station

P.S. I have kept my eye open for our family friend, but little gets on or off the Rock these days.

<hr />

21 January 1805

Ashton

My father is Dead—I cannot bear it! I have spent the day writing to my family. I have composed each letter with the proper degree of melancholy and restraint. I have reviewed for them his last hours and the remedies we tried. I have painted a picture of a quiet decline and a peaceful departure. I lied. It was blow after blow, a respite to embolden our hopes, then another ugly blow. After the first rounds of fever he got up and had a quiet evening. He ate breakfast as usual. He was weak, as everyone is after such a bout, but he passed the day in light reading and quiet rest. He was getting better and then suddenly he was dead. How could he worsen so rapidly and die so quickly?

I wrote everyone that we had a thousand shared comforts in our memories, but I lied again. Memory is an evil ghost compared to living flesh. How could he die and leave us alone, the kindest and gentlest man I ever knew? I informed the family that he passed quietly, "almost in his sleep." But death is neither quiet nor peaceful. It was a brutal murder. Death strangled my father. *I am sick of everyone dying that I care about. I cannot stop weeping. I cry blood. I want to stab someone in the eye. The world must suffer, it must.*

Jane

———✦———

13 May 1805

Dear Jane

The pain you are feeling causes me to put aside the conventional comments of a friend to someone grieving. Polite words of sympathy never help, except to acknowledge that the person is aware of one's loss. I wish to express my concern as plainly as possible. I am profoundly grieved to hear of your loss. Your family's loss. I wish I had been present in England to pay my respects—proper, personal respects. Not condolence by formula. Your father was the best of men, evidenced by the fine family he has left behind and by the despair contained within your letter.

Though our families reconciled after the balloon adventure, I regret that he and I never met again. The last time I saw your father was on the day of my Chastisement—the day I began to grow up. No reprimand has ever had on me the effect of your father's. My own father's discipline always had the objective of preparing me for the responsibilities that I would undertake as heir to the family fortune. His scrutiny was so severe as to make many people, myself among the rest, wonder whether he loved me. He did not seem to want to make me a good man so much as he wanted to make me a prudent custodian of his wealth. His interest seemed commercial rather than parental, if I make sense.

But when your *father confronted me, I saw something I had never seen before. His anger was not at having had his family's reputation besmirched or a prize possession put at risk. His very real emotion—frank and brutal words—rose from the finest sort of love. For his daughter and* her very soul.

I did not know that such disinterested love could exist. It took your father's censure, followed by your rejection of me and the quiet reflection of two years on the Rock (including, I must add, the experience of death and suffering around me), to help me to understand what loves means. Love is not a passion or a personal attachment. These are merely symptoms. Love is an obligation—joyously accepted—to gain the respect and affection of the people around you each and every day. Love is not what you crave but what you earn. *As your father did. As Captain Maurice has done in a radically different situation here—parallels your father's in ways I understand even if I cannot explain them.*

Seeing your father's anguish over you did open my eyes to the fact that my own father's love must have run deeper than I ever gave him credit for. I resented his assumption that I would become a rogue out of a ladies' novel. I had given him no reason to believe that I would become irresponsible, but I also had given him no evidence to the contrary. His unrelenting correction on the tiniest deviation of my behavior was his way of trying to penetrate adolescent intransigence. I now understand—somewhat better— the panic he must have felt over the harm I might bring upon my mother and sisters through recklessness—the sort of recklessness that you yourself have experienced. He must have loved me to have insisted so fiercely on my maturity.

This slow—painful—development of insight began with my Chastisement at the hands of Mr. Austen.

Your father taught me to love my father, if not as warmly as you do yours. I know what I mean even if I make no sense to you. Can I express any finer compliment about Mr. Austen to the daughter who grieves so wretchedly?

I confess, finally, that your father's love for you was a precipitating factor in my intemperate proposal to you. My regard was honest, if immature, but the depth of affection that runs throughout your family gave me an inkling of the happiness that real love must encompass—not just your father's for you, but his love for your mother, your love for your sister, your mother's for her children, all of you for one another. I selfishly sought to possess that affection for myself before I in any way knew how to deserve it.

My words are like a rockslide off the cliff. I hope they do no damage.
I put at risk the equanimity that now exists between us with this frank
confession, but it is the only way I know to express my understanding of
the agony you feel over your father's death and the ragged hole it must leave
in your heart. I grieve for you, Jane. I grieve for your grief—

Ashton
HMS Diamond Rock
North American Station

⚜

12 June 1805

Dear Cass

 Attached is a letter that arrived by yesterday's post. The letter exhibited
the crumpled, dispirited look that we identify with the damp missives from
our distant brothers, but the handwriting is neither Frank's nor Charles'.
You will know instantly whose letter it must be. Though you were dubious
about the correspondence, you have been discreet enough in the last two and
a half years not to reprimand me for the occasional exchanges. The topic
is usually a matter of interest to the Herschels or another colleague in the
field of natural philosophy. Because of the difficulty of mail from the West
Indies, he has chosen to use a single conduit, a role I have been happy to
serve considering the rapprochement we have had with the Dennis family.
 My last letter to him naturally included the news of Father's death.
The enclosed letter is his reply. After reading it, I had to put it aside until
late in the evening, when I read it again. I read it again today twice over.
I do not know what to say to him in return. Indeed, I have no idea what
to say at all.
 What do you think of this letter, which I have copied out and enclosed?

Yr sister,
J. Austen

⚜

14 June 1805

Dear Jane

I think we should have said yes—and meant it.

Yr sister,
C. Austen

———❦———

21 June 1805

Dear Ashton

I have not been able to compose a reply to your generous letter of 13 May because it occasioned so many emotions that I did not know how to respond. Even now I do not know what to say except that I treasure it. Come home.

Jane

———❦———

27 June 1805

Dear Sister

As the family's banker, I have repeatedly assured Mother that the women in the family have nothing to fear regarding their maintenance as a consequence of Father's death. Yet I have still another letter from Mother worrying over finances—a composition that I am sure she slipped into the post without your awareness, or Cassandra's. This letter confirms that the Austen family will all provide the necessary supplements to enable Mother, and of course you and Cass, to live in a manner close to that which has been possible in the years since Father's retirement.

I send the information to you and Cassandra as a matter of record because, in her bereavement, Mother has continued to forget what we have agreed upon—or remembers incorrectly—and consequently has experienced one bout of despondency after another as she contemplates her future. I know this has been a trial for you and Cassandra.

Should she suffer any more despair over circumstances, please show her this letter as an official reminder of the following: Mother has approximately 140 pounds of income a year. Edward will contribute 100 pounds (which will include his clothing allowance for you sisters). Frank, James, and I will contribute 50 pounds each. Frank offered to match Edward's contribution, but his generosity outstrips his means. Mother, I know, will politely decline if he sends anything more than 50. Because Charles is so young and his naval career just under way, he has not been asked to contribute; that expectation will change as the years advance. Cassandra has the income from Tom Fowle's bequest (would that this generous man could see the value of his thoughtfulness today!). In total, you should all have a living of approximately 440 pounds per annum.

You will be full rich as ever! I have every confidence that Mother will have all those comforts which her declining years and precarious health call for. It was wise of her to reduce her establishment to one female domestic and take furnished lodgings, as a smaller establishment will be agreeable to you all. Sometime in the next year or two it will likely make sense for you to move from Bath, to be closer to the rest of us so that we can more easily assist in other ways. This is not a matter to discuss with Mother now, as the thought of leaving her beloved Bath would further increase her distraction.

Y loving brother,*
Henry

---

30 June 1805

Dear Sister

What I am about to recount will be public knowledge by the time you receive this letter. Indeed, you must be aware of the first part already. The French fleet, under Villeneuve, escaped our blockade of the Channel and made its way to the West Indies, there to pillage our shipping and supply lines. Despite Villeneuve having seized an advantage of several weeks, Lord Nelson gathered his own fleet and gave chase the instant he knew of Villeneuve's destination. Villeneuve recognized that French domination here was impossible so long as the British flag flew above Diamond Rock. *He launched an immediate, massive attack, including two first-raters carrying seventy-four guns each: a total of* sixteen *ships.*

The following information has been distributed to the Fleet and to the local British community by Lord Nelson. The first is a letter from Captain Maurice of HMS Diamond Rock *in which he recounts the attack by the combined French and Spanish fleets. The* Diamond Rock *endured two weeks of blockade followed by several days of severe combat. I do not wish to alarm you, for beyond Maurice's letter we have no other information about casualties or the fate of his crew. I will let you know the instant I hear.*

"MY LORD

"IT is with the greatest sorrow I have to inform you of the loss of the Diamond Rock, under my command, which was obliged to surrender on the 2nd inst., after three days' attack from a squadron of two sail of the line, one frigate, one brig, a schooner, eleven gun-boats and, from the nearest calculation, 1500 troops. The want of ammunition and water was the sole occasion of its unfortunate loss. ... Our losses were only two killed and one wounded. The enemy, from the nearest account I have been able to obtain, lost on shore 30 killed and 40 wounded: they also lost three gun-boats and two rowing boats."

The second enclosure is an excerpt that I have written out summarizing the results of Captain Maurice's court martial. I am sure you know that a trial is mandatory after a captain has lost a ship—the Rock, *in this case. Personally, I commend the Captain for his resolve to defend the island for as long as it was feasible, and for his willingness to save his crew when he had no way to carry on. We know that the crew was taken to Fort-de-France—the very port they had effectively blockaded these many months—but we do not know their fate after that. All we know is that he had more than a hundred men.*

"The Court is of the opinion that Captain J.W. Maurice, the Officers and Company of His Majesty's late sloop Diamond Rock did every thing in their power to the very last, in the defence of the Rock, and against a most superior force. ... [Because Maurice] did not surrender the Diamond until he was unable to make further defence for want of water and ammunition, the Court do therefore honorably acquit Captain Maurice accordingly."

Jane, I am sure you are concerned about Mr. Dennis, but the small number of casualties bodes well. I write in haste for fear that any delay will cause you to hear only that the Rock *has been lost after a great battle. No doubt such news would cause you anxiety in the extreme. It is likely that*

Mr. Dennis is safe and will be repatriated, though of course we cannot be sure when this will happen. You may wish to alert the Dennis family, in the most sensitive manner possible, of the circumstances.

You should take heart, too, that the time wasted in the attack on Diamond Rock *has been of enormous benefit to our cause. The delay gave Nelson time to catch up, putting Villeneuve at a profound disadvantage, squeezed between the fleets of both Nelson and Hood. Seeing that he was now vastly overmatched, the French admiral immediately set sail for home. Except for a merchantman or two that blundered across his path, Villeneuve's crossing of the Atlantic was to absolutely no avail. HMS* Diamond Rock's *stubborn resistance has prevented the invasion of the British West Indies and set back the French Navy by many months.*

Frank, of course, was with Nelson's fleet on the Canopus. *They arrived two days after Maurice was forced to surrender. Nelson, along with Frank, has already given chase—again!—after Villeneuve. The fleet barely had time to resupply before sailing back to Europe. There was no opportunity for me to see my brother.*

I shall write when I know more.

Yr loving brother,
C. Austen
HMS Indian
North American Station

———

Part III

Autumn 1805

Chapter 20

"I confess to being tired of these unplanned journeys to and from the Dennis house," Cassandra said. "We should seek a constable escort."

"The other visits were emotional," Jane said, glancing out of the carriage without really seeing the landscape. "But they were not important. Not important in any deep sense of the word."

Charles' letter had interrupted an extended visit at Godmersham with Edward and his family. Godmersham, in Kent, was nearly twice as far from Hants as Bath, in Somerset. They were fortunate that Edward was willing to dispatch them immediately with outriders for an escort. Reaching the White Horse Inn in Dorking (the only place Edward would consider having them stop for the night) had taken multiple changes of horse and Edward's coachman pushing each pair until they staggered. Under favorable conditions the carriage ride to or from Godmersham was one of their favorites, and they had once spent a pleasurable week in Surrey that began with a hunt for rare orchids and ended with a picnic on one of its inviting green hills. This time, however, banging along behind the flying pair, Jane barely noticed any of the county's scenery.

She calmed the worst of her fears by telling herself that it was unlikely for Ashton to have been harmed. Two men dead, one injured, out of a party of a hundred. Ashton was not a regular combatant. Like as not, he was well out of the way, guarding the goats and chickens. Of course that was not true. Even as a civilian, he would not have been far from the front line. His pride would have compelled him forward, and he had at least theoretical command of some of the men. He would have been close, at the very least helping with supplies, filling in wherever help was needed. But only three casualties. One could not complain about the Rock having had only three casualties. She said a short prayer for the three; not because one might have been Ashton but because, if none of them were Ashton, she did not wish to diminish their importance.

As they jolted along, her thoughts shifted to the question of his return. After nearly three years, much of it on an isolated island, she had no doubt that he would soon be bound for England. He had not spent his time entertaining colonial women after all, she thought. The emotion in his letters had become so urgent that she knew any reason at all would have had him fly to her. That thought arrested her. Did she feel so entitled? Was she that presumptuous? Did she even *want* him to fly to her? Had she not, at least indirectly, sent him away? Had he not left to rid himself of his ties to her? Or was the departure really to enlarge his soul so that he would be worthy of her—his way of thinking, not hers. It was more likely that he wanted to enlarge his soul to pursue any number of other interests—and other women. If he returned a man, would he want her? Would she now want him? If he returned a man, would she be worthy of *him*? She in truth did not understand their relationship, or how they would react to each other when they met again face to face.

It was possible that the closeness they had achieved by letter was unique to the circumstance of loneliness and distance. What if all they still had in person was his stuttering rudeness and her clever superiority? She had to wonder how much a youth could become a man in less than three years. True, he had left at the cusp of maturity, those few critical years when a young man either slides back into childish things or steps fully into adulthood. He had seen a new world, islands and seas she could hardly imagine. He had faced privation. He had seen war, though until the last week, barely anything that would count. (Does it make any difference if it is a dozen musket balls whizzing by your head, or a thousand?) Frank and Charles had both returned changed men after their very first combat at sea.

"She cannot have heard," Cassandra mused. Alethea would have written and urged them to come and await the news if she had received any communication about *Diamond Rock*.

"The kindest thing is if we are the first to tell her," Jane responded. They had discussed at least a dozen times in the day and a half on the road the importance of Alethea hearing the news from them rather than from someone else. Cassandra's comment was what they said to each other when they both became too miserable in their thoughts.

Who was this Ashton that, she had to believe, would be home soon? This was the question that troubled her. Yes, she was worried that he might be dead. But death was a finality that could not be encompassed until the worst was actually known. If he were alive, he was bound to return to Hampshire. She tried to dissuade herself from the likelihood that she really was just a convenient correspondent, the one woman he could write with no more stain on his reputation than what had already set. He wrote to her because he could; they became close because it was inevitable. One had to believe that that closeness had not been solely the result of Ashton's isolation. Yet she feared that their intimacy would be abandoned on the Rock along with the wrecked guns and camp equipment.

Jane pondered again his last letter, its brashness, its embarrassing frankness. He spoke the truth about her family's affections, something which she took for granted but which was rare enough in the many families of their acquaintance. She remained unsettled by the letter's passion. Even now she could not say whether the feelings were for her father, for her loss, or for her. He wrote with the guileless emotion of someone who has downed half a bottle of wine, yet she knew that alcohol was the one thing he handled with care. Perhaps living on an isolated rock with a small group of confederates magnified his feelings or caused him to lose the perspective of how one spoke in regular society.

No. The letter was Ashton being Ashton, preferring to say what he thought. Not what people thought he ought to say.

She preferred those honest, chaotic feelings, even if they bordered upon the inappropriate, to the litany of piety and meaningless nothings about her father that had accumulated in the weeks of personal visits and in the letters that still arrived. In almost all the commiseration, even from the dearest of friends and family, the words could have applied to the death of any decent man. Only Ashton's words were particular to her father. Only Ashton seemed to know her father and to understand Jane's loss at his death. Given that he barely knew her father, it was most likely that Ashton identified so intensely with *her* that he felt her pain as his own. She was not sure whether this was good or bad. Ashton was the only person, except for Cassandra, who spoke to her without any shielding from the heart's depth. Why should that offend her or, indeed, anyone?

She had read the letter again and again until she could nearly recite it from memory; it was in her bag even now. She put it aside for a week or two, and upon re-reading became electrified again by his emotions and their implications. Had he reminded her of his proposal in the hopes that he might renew his quest? Would she remain opposed? If Ashton did want her, was she ready? Or had she, in the female corollary, herself fallen back into childish things? More likely she was too old, too afraid, to take the risk of an adult life with an adult male. She was not even certain that she could weather and return his passion once it was directed solely and intimately at her. Regardless of suitor, she feared that she had missed the window of early womanhood, when the excitement of the unknown carried females into relationships that common sense and discretion might otherwise tell them to avoid. And of course there was the final fear, the vanity. Ashton was three years more the man. She was three years more the spinster. Dear Lord, at year's end she would be thirty!

For the most part these were not the conscious, well-ordered thoughts of her usual deliberation. They were waves of sentiment and flashes of memory, colored by snatches of phrases from their letters, stirred by the thoughts and intimacies they had shared in word, agitated by the knowledge that she might be conjecturing about a man who was dead or badly wounded. As pleasing as some of them were, these thoughts existed in the world of her own private fancy. That would-be life had its own flow, its own worries, and its own future, but it never impinged in any way on her actual reality. She was now the daughter of an impecunious widow. They would live on her mother's and sister's tiny incomes and on the annual supplements from her brothers; they would travel on the whim and generosity of others. Daydreams never caused her to lose sight of the sober exterior world. The interior view, being her own, was one that she could simultaneously enjoy and ignore. It was an outcome as unlikely to happen as her winning thirty thousand pounds in the English state lottery, yet no less enjoyable to anticipate.

Cassandra sat staring out of the window, nearly as preoccupied as Jane, who recognized that Cass's thoughts must inevitably drift toward Tom and his death in the Caribbean. Was Jane replicating Cassandra's experience? Were the two sisters destined to parallel one another's unhappiness all their lives? Even here she was being presumptuous. Cassy had been engaged; Jane had refused an engagement. Yet an understanding with Ashton had developed, undefined as it might be.

From her worry and confusion, few thoughts bubbled up coherently to the surface of her mind. The only intelligible expression that repeated in her consciousness was more canticle than commentary: Come home to me, Ashton. Come home.

Hants House was close now. Houses, fields, stands of oaks and elms were all familiar. They ought to be experiencing an increase in tension or worry. But exhaustion was complete from the ride and from twenty-four nonstop hours of apprehension. All of them—Jane, Cassandra, and the coachman—were stiff and sore. The concern, the fear, was there, deep and solid, but its finish was dull and flat. The unknown was there to be faced, that was all.

Finally, broken clouds gave way and Hants House suddenly appeared as if it had stepped out into the view to take a bit of sun. Through the years, the sight had affected her many different ways. As a child, she had been intimidated by the three-story wall of buff brick, as wide as the horizon. As she grew older, she found the rambling pile comforting and was disappointed when Ashton's father began the massive enterprise to regularize and improve the home. It was, she realized later, one of the few "improvements" that had in fact improved both the appearance and the functionalism of an historic wreck. A white brick trim and white brick entrance now pulled the buff brick house visually together. The new two-story entrance stepped out welcomingly from the main three-story house. The set of rounded arches in the entrance softened the line of rectangular windows that marched across the house. Four statues above the entrance (unusual for the time but somehow satisfying) indicated that this was a home rather than a fortress. These renovations, done in the late 1780s, had established Hants as the preeminent house in Hampshire, well beyond that of Highclere, further west, and equal to Langhorne, home of the Earl of Solent, in the south. (There was something about Langhorne she should recall, but her agitation prevented the recovery of the memory.)

Jane's strongest and fondest memories, of course, were her arrivals for the balls. The broad shoulders of the brick house, fronted by the meadow, the brook, and the huge expanse of lawn, bespoke entertainment, frivolity, and the chance of flirtation. Not merely flirtation with a boy, but with life. The ball represented the glittering possibilities of the future. More than once, she had entertained the vision of Hants House one day being hers—no actual man was ever attached to that dream. Eventually, of course, the dream had faded.

Hants House became a synecdoche for all the impressive castles, estates, mansions and country homes over which she would never preside. Today, the lack of activity around the house bode ill, as if the news about Ashton had already arrived. She recognized that she was projecting her own emptiness, suspending her emotion to maintain a reserve against the worst.

They were taken straight to the sitting-room, and Alethea rose to greet them warmly. At each visit she seemed ever so slightly rounder. She is a woman, Jane thought, who by forty should be as full as a pudding, with a fond and equally plump husband and a swarm of laughing children. Even now there was a brightness that made Jane immediately think—a man! As she ordered tea and settled them into comfortable chairs, Alethea smiled as if she had a secret to share.

"It is so good of you to come," Alethea said. "A letter is on the table, waiting for the post, to invite you down."

"How is Mrs. Dennis?" Jane inquired.

"Asleep. After the *excitement* of this morning, I doubt that we will hear from her till dinner."

Jane was too distracted to much register the emphasis of the word *excitement*. Alethea had answered one question, though, which was how to handle the news if there were the risk of Mrs. Dennis elbowing in partway through.

"We have had a communication," Jane said, anxiously exchanging a glance with Cassandra. Jane had a natural delicacy in announcing unpleasant news—an illness, a death—but she was at a loss now. Alethea meant too much to her, and knew her too well, for her to come at the news about Ashton in a roundabout way. At the same time, she feared the brutality of the frank disclosure.

"About Mr. Dennis," Cassandra injected after the silence extended for a heartbeat too long. "Ashton," she added, as if the formal address might still create confusion with his late father.

"Then you have heard!" Alethea exclaimed with a laugh that echoed through the large, bright room. "Of course," she said, clapping her hands. "Your brother must have written."

Jane and Cassandra looked at each other in bewilderment. Surely Charles had not written to Alethea. He would know that they would rush to her. He would know that they would soften the blow as much as possible. He would not have preempted them, particularly with news of such import.

"Yes," Jane said. She had Charles' letter in her hand. No matter how many times she had read it, the news had not changed. Her explanation of the attack, the fall of the Rock, and the dispersal and disappearance of the crew, she thought, would be the opening barrage. The letter would be the final assault.

"Then you know about *Diamond Rock*?" Cassandra said.

"How bravely they fought against impossible odds?" Jane said.

"Until they ran out of ammunition?" Cassandra added.

"Yes, yes," Alethea said, continuing to beam. "Your brother told it in stirring detail. A battle for the ages! A hundred men against the French fleet! Smoke and powder! Shot flying! A fight to the bitter end!" She sounded positively intoxicated. "I cannot tell you how grateful we are to Captain Austen," she added. "All that he has done for us. What a fine officer!"

Tea arrived. Alethea helped herself to the sweet cake. Jane and Cass were even more perplexed than a few moments before. Even if Charles had written her, he would not have trumpeted the battle. He would have written very much as he had to Jane, praising the men's courage in that cautious British way as a salve against the possibility of Ashton's death or grave harm.

"It was very kind of him to write," Jane said, feeling her way along. "He explained everything to us—as apparently he did to you. But I am puzzled at your *elation* at the news." She half-heartedly held out Charles' letter, not sure what to do with it.

It was Alethea's turn to express bewilderment. "How could I not feel elation?"

"Of course!" Cassandra inserted. "Charles heard! He found out that Ashton was fine and wrote directly. That would have been the fastest and most sympathetic thing! There will be a letter for us when we get home, surely."

The two sisters let out cries of relief.

"You have heard? Ashton was not hurt?" Jane said.

Alethea set down her tea. "Of course he was hurt. Who said anything about Charles? It was Frank who wrote."

Jane's cup rattled in her hand, though she was able to get it to the table without dropping anything to the floor. "*Badly* hurt?" What has Frank got to do with it, she thought. And why would Frank, who barely knew the Dennises, have written to Alethea? Whatever he had heard about the battle, at most he would have penned a line to his sisters.

Realization spread across Alethea's face. "You do not know!" She leaned back, laughing disconcertingly loud while clapping her hands again, and pulled a letter from the book she had been reading. After making a show of unfolding the pages, Alethea read the introductory passages to herself. "The recounting of the battle was actually quite factual," she said aloud. "I must have inserted the fireworks myself. Ah, here we are."

Her voice changed to the tone that a man would use to make an official announcement: "I am pleased to report that HMS *Canopus* picked up nineteen of the crew of HMS *Diamond Rock*, including one who was wounded. Eighteen men, all sailors before the mast, were transferred to a British ship that would remain in the West Indies. The injured party, a civilian who had taken on irregular duties with Captain Maurice, asked to return with the *Canopus* to England. I told the civilian, a Mr. Dennis, that the ship and crew were likely to see hot action in pursuit of the French before reaching port. Upon Mr. Dennis noting that he had recent acquaintance with hot action and would assist as much as he was able, according to his injury, I accepted his request to remain aboard as a gentleman passenger."

Here Alethea broke off with a look that seemed to ask whether the contents were in the least bit familiar to them. "Continue," Jane said. Cass sat impassively. Alethea was now playing with them, and neither sister intended to give her the pleasure of watching the Austens squirm.

"Mr. Dennis had suffered a gunshot wound to the jaw. Our initial conversation was oral on my part and written on his. However, Mr. Dennis did well in the hands of the surgeon, and the wound healed during the weeks at sea. I found great pleasure in his company, particularly once I made the connection with the Dennis family of Hants House. We shared many fine memories of growing up in Hampshire. Being that the fleet did not find Villeneuve before reaching home, the *Canopus* put in for resupply, and Mr. Dennis was registered with the hospital in Portsmouth."

Jane flew from her chair. "We must go! Why are you here? Why are you not with your brother?"

"I *am* with my brother, Jane," Alethea said. "Please forgive me. I thought you knew. I assumed you had heard from Frank—why you had come. I did not mean to be cruel. Please."

Alethea took Jane and Cassandra by the hand and led them to the large rear window. The view extended past the small garden directly behind the house, past the stables and a pond, and toward the newly mown fields sweeping off toward the distance.

Jane's eye caught the scene in its entirety; but, unable to believe its full meaning, and its potential effect on her life, her mind rebelled. In order to comprehend the overall prospect before her, she had to step through and make sense of each element, deliberately and in turn. What registered first was the hot-air balloon. Hovering in the sky with its ludicrous designs, the aerostat reminded her for some reason of a giant jester's face. From the basket leaned the steward, Mr. Fletcher. Halfway between the balloon and the ground, slung by a set of ropes, hung a large bewildered cow. On the ground were half a dozen farm hands tending another set of ropes; steering the balloon, these men displayed an amused, uncommitted attitude as if they had been asked to do something that must conclude in disappointment. This task appeared to be the relocation of the cow, whose legs were beating as if the beast were trying to assist.

Finally she perceived an image that, even as she feared for its ephemerality, resolved into unquestionable solidity. On the side of the field opposite the other men stood a figure as straight and rigid as a statue, legs wide apart like a colossus. It was a tall, broad, dark-haired man. He was gesticulating, as if trying to demonstrate to the workers and the cow the complicated mechanics of flight.

Chapter 21

Mrs. Dennis came down a few hours later. She must have been told of Jane and Cassandra's arrival because she exhibited no surprise at their presence. In the way of inoculation, Alethea immediately told her mother that the Austens had heard only of the capture of *Diamond Rock*, not of Ashton's return. "They came to keep me company until we knew the worst," she said, reaching out to take Cassandra's hand to imply that the visit came at the instigation of the older sister.

Mrs. Dennis nodded and exchanged the usual courtesies and ordered dinner to be served. The ladies engaged in the chit-chat that fills the time while one waits for something to happen.

Ashton strode in a quarter of an hour later, punctual but finding that dinner was already under way. The sound of his boots (perhaps his most definitive signature) and the movement of his shadow announced his progress down the hall. He entered the room in his standard dress from years before: light jacket, yellow breeches, and grimed Hessian boots. Once he would have strode into the room as if intending to knock down a wall, but today Ashton entered with more restraint, as if reserving his aggression for a wall that actually warranted punishment. The younger women rose to greet him. He took everyone in with a glance, expressed pleasure, kissed his mother's hand and his sister's cheek, and greeted the Austen sisters with the proper decorum. As he swept toward Jane, both he and she seemed to flex, like two magnetic objects that approached unexpectedly within the other's range. The pull—and the resistance to it—was so subtle and the moment so brief that only the keenest observer would have noticed; but all the ladies were tuned to the slightest variation in emotional currents. His dark eyes contained neither desire nor eagerness, but sparkled with genuine happiness;

it was a feeling that Jane shared and hoped also to shine in her own eyes. Their restraint measured a growth in maturity, she thought. Impulsivity is not a lack of control per se but a natural response to the state of ambiguity. When one knows something is going to happen, it is not necessary for it to happen ill-advisedly. The calmness with which they greeted each other told her instantly that what had grown between them through correspondence was real. They were the dearest of friends. If that was all they were, she felt the richer for it. She was not entirely collected, though. Her emotions were not so much in control as in perspective.

"Oh dear," she said, referring to the red welt that ran along the left side of his face from his lip to the bottom of his ear. It was shocking but somehow not unpleasant. She registered not the scar but how much worse the injury could have easily been. In contrast to that possibility, this was a fortunate scratch. By altering the shape and proportions of his aspect, the welt also brought the planes of his face together, creating more of a whole than before. For the first time, Jane felt that she could *see* Ashton.

"Frank's letter arrived in the last post," Alethea reported excitedly. "We sent Mr. Fletcher ahead to give us time to organize an expedition, and he came upon Ashton on the road early this morning." Alethea beamed at her brother with pride: He had found himself in a war, acquitted himself well, and come home safe. He had also, with one stroke, so to speak, redefined himself. He was no longer the reckless, ill-tempered youth who experimented with embarrassment. His mark of courage and responsibility outweighed any earlier peccadilloes. *That scar? He won it against the French.* "Perhaps Ashton will tell you how he received his wound," Alethea said. "He has been silent on the issue with us."

"I violated a basic tenet of warfare," Ashton replied. "Never peek over the parapet when someone is shooting at you."

"It must have been terribly painful," Cassandra said.

Ashton shrugged. "The French assault was so violent that it was not possible to hear one's own thoughts. After days of bombardment we were all numb. One moment I was fine and the next moment I was under the surgeon's care. Captain Maurice said my head snapped around and I said something like 'how very odd.' What must have taken several minutes to bring me down to one of the cots seemed to have happened instantly. I remember the sailors who helped me. I recall Maurice checking on me. All the important moments; nothing in between. Imagine if time were a deck of cards in which everything but the face cards have been removed. That is how compressed everything felt. The rest of the battle receded into the distance. I awoke the next day with a terrible headache. Kept on for some time." He was silent for a moment. "I was fortunate that the injury happened near the end. That is another rule I violated. Never take a risk when you know there will be a parlay."

"What a relief that you had medical care aboard the *Canopus*," Jane said.

He nodded. "Frank did not recognize me at first, and I was not forthcoming because of the laudanum. It was several days before we made the connection. Your brother is an officer's officer. Not a wasted word or motion. No silly work for the crew, but in every spare moment an exercise to ready them for battle. Too quiet to exhibit the charm of the rest of the family, but humorous in his own way. A capital fellow."

"They call him the officer who kneels at church," Jane said. "His propriety on deck and in church is not for show. It is who he is. When he was a boy, we called him *Fly*. He was all energy and joy. He may have been the most sensitive of us all. Much like his father. I am afraid that the rigors of naval school on a twelve-year-old boy, and his many years of service, have caused him to close upon himself. Unless he is with family."

"The Navy does well to take recklessness out of youth, for there are no old, reckless sailors," Ashton said. "Captain Austen is not as harsh a disciplinarian as most captains. But even moderate Navy discipline is severe by ordinary standards. Your brother has made a conscious choice to be as he is. It will keep him and his crew alive. He is like Maurice in that way. Even if it costs Frank the elevated spirits of his siblings. This is my observation. I am not an expert."

They were quiet for a few minutes. "Your mention of your father, the late Mr. Austen, reminds me that I have not formally expressed my condolences," Ashton said. "Please let me express my sympathy on behalf of myself and the Dennis family. Mr. Austen was a good man. Please pay our respects to Mrs. Austen. I know it has been many months. Your affairs are likely all in order. But if there *is* anything we can do, please do not hesitate to ask." He spoke in exactly the right tone, sympathetic without being sentimental, formal without being brusque—not formulaic, is that the word he had used? It was as if his earlier letter had drained the excess of emotion from his heart, enabling him to modulate his expression in a manner ordinarily beyond his reach.

"You are too kind, sir," Cassandra replied on behalf of both of them.

Chapter 22

Jane, Cassandra, and Alethea were enjoying the brisk air the next day in the big garden when Ashton appeared from a side path, took Jane's arm, and pivoted her in a new direction. The move was far smoother than she had ever seen him make on the dance floor. Alethea deftly pulled along Cassandra, who was surprised but did not protest, and they quickly disappeared. Jane and Ashton walked in comfortable silence for some time. It seemed enough for them to let their thoughts and emotions reorder themselves around the many changes in circumstances since their last walk together, so long ago. It was as if old pieces of a puzzle had to be rearranged, and new pieces had to be cut, in order for them to find coherence in the pattern in which they now found themselves.

"I am pleased to be home," he said. "Living on the Rock in a military encampment was not as romantic as it may have appeared from my letters. There were not nearly enough dances."

Listening to his words and examining his expressions, she felt a certain incongruity, the result of his authentic presence replacing the projection of his self from words written on the page. We feel how much we love only when we meet again, she thought. Yet the meeting requires that we adjust our perceptions, to deal with crisp actuality rather than softly focused supposition.

"I enjoyed your letters," she said. "When expressed by pen, your sentiments come through unimpeded."

"Lieutenant Maurice is not here to assist. Should I send for him?"

"Your letters were your own. I could hear your voice, *distilled* I would say."

"Without my sarcasm and stammer, you mean."

"I much prefer a flawed presence to a perfect absence."

"*Susan?*" he asked hurriedly, as if embarrassed by her remark. For an instant she thought he meant a person but then understood his reference to the novel. Her vehement negative shake of the head shut the door on any further inquiry.

"It feels like a holiday," she said. "Since we saw you in the field. Knowing you were safe."

The weather remained fine, though an occasional chill gust warned of approaching change. Trees clung to their summer greens, yet a perceptible tint to the shimmering leaves portended the beginning of autumn. Jane and Ashton wound along in one of the more curious sections of the estate. Hants House had been a working farm long before it became a grand family home, so there was no formal garden expounding from behind the mansion. There was just a splash of color from a few small flower beds to soothe the eye of sir and madam when they surveyed their holdings. The large formal garden had instead been built on the side of the building, to the north. The original had been done in the customary Versailles style by the aristocratic family that had owned Hants House for more than two hundred years. As if to make up for the unorthodox placement, the garden was twice the size of any that Jane had seen. It contained rows of bright annuals and perennials, fountains and statues, and long runs of small rectangular shrubs interspersed by tall topiary in elaborate styles.

The late Mr. Dennis had added an intricate maze of hedgerows and a park into which the hedgerows debouched. This park was done in the more natural English landscape style that had overtaken the French design in popularity. Asymmetrical arrangements of oak, birch, and mountain ash merged together like a well-composed landscape painting, framing the obligatory view of an Ionic temple across the obligatory lake. Built to look as though it had been there since the time of ancient Greece, the temple sat atop a small rise behind the lake to create a focal point on the horizon. Ashton and Jane had met in the labyrinth of hedgerows, which enabled a lengthy private walk in a relatively small area, and eventually made their way around the lake and up the rise to the temple. There they sat, an agreeable view of the Hants House holdings to the south and of the farms scattered across the verdant valley to the north.

Alone, Jane felt no qualms about reaching up toward the red streak across his face. She did not touch him. She contoured his face in the air, as if the concern she felt was too sensitive for physical involvement. He smiled an uncommitted smile.

"You have all that you need?" he said. "For your stay?"

"Of course. Though we did not expect to be dressing for a ball. We had to send to Edward for a trunk of suitable clothes."

"Return of the prodigal son. My mother cannot miss the opportunity. To put me on display as soon as possible."

"For the next Miss Stanley," Jane said. The first one had married in the year after Ashton's departure.

"I understand what society thinks of rough men such as my father. And I. We are society's short men: The aristocracy looks down their nose at us. Yet because we are rich, at every ball and dinner I am examined by the women like a cut of beef by a roomful of butchers. Not only am I to be greedily consumed by anyone with the proper pedigree, I am to provide the expensive cutlery with which I am to be carved up and the silver plate on which I am to be served. ..."

Once Ashton would have worked himself up into wrath over the commercial aspects of betrothal, but today he seemed bemused rather than bitter, as if the bother would not last much longer. That topic, Ashton's availability for marriage, might have led to a discourse on their own relationship. In his silence, she watched to see if his face would reveal a desire to delve more deeply, if only for clarity as to where they stood with each other. There was nothing.

"Your mother is well?" he asked after an interval.

"She is dismayed at having to eventually leave Bath, though she understands as well as anyone the necessity. Our brothers are making arrangements. It is not clear where we will finally alight. It is good we enjoy traveling."

This too—the need for Jane to find a permanent residence—might have stimulated the opening of the conversation that she knew they needed to have, a conversation that she felt Ashton also knew they needed to have. Indeed, should want to have. Yet again, silence. Yet again, nothing on his face to indicate a desire to really talk; nothing to show either uncertain feelings or any kind of a decision.

"I am sure they will look out for you, your brothers," he said. "Edward in particular has the resources."

She surveyed the expanse before her, now beginning to settle into twilight. Lamps and fires from the many farmhouses cast a flickering glow like fireflies well off into the distance. The evening star shone forth in the west, and two others nearby wavered into view like freshly lit candles. The moon peeked over the far trees as if to ensure that the sun had really set before venturing into the sky. There was the lowing of cattle, all in succession; the hay was out, she was sure they were saying. There was the happy bark of a dog on the run; she suspected a chase with a child doing the last of the day's chores. There was an eruption of laughter by laborers in the distance as they headed home to sup. A brag or a naughty story to hold off the good earned hunger of working men. She breathed deeply. The air had that delectable coolness in which a couple on familiar terms might find warmth in the nearness of the other. If there were any time for a man to speak to a woman, this was it. Yet he sat mute. Eyes fixed on the dirt floor of the temple in which they sat. Unaware, it seemed, of anything Jane saw. Or felt. Ashton's feelings, which in every other situation were fully on display, were absent. Or buried so deep they would not come out.

Perhaps, Jane thought, he said nothing because he had nothing to say. She wondered whether they had put so much into their letters that there was nothing more for them to tell each other. Yet for her the correspondence had been just a taste of what they might be together. How could two people become so close and not venture further? If *this* were not going to happen, surely an explanation was in order. Surely he owed her that much. He could acknowledge his feelings yet say that, upon seeing her again after so much time, he no longer found her attractive in the marriageable way. Or that after three more years, she was simply too old. Perhaps he felt that any such mention might insult her further than he usually did. Yet this silence was too much. An understood silence was sweet. A separate silence was bitter. His fate was to marry well. Her fate was to be part of a traveling female circus, entertaining relatives for their keep. This was of course the most logical outcome, the most expected, the most probable.

She took in again the expanse of land and sky. It was as beautiful as a few moments before, but it had lost its inspiration. It no longer felt like the universe around them but a dim glass bowl. But something *was* there between them, Jane and Ashton. Stop any woman on the street and give her one of his letters to read and she would say: *This man loves you.* One could not reach any other conclusion. Yet here he sat, unspeaking. It was over, she suddenly thought. Nothing was going to happen. The moment, whatever it was that Jane had imagined it to be, however much she had expanded it with expectancy, had passed.

One assumed that people acted because of what they felt. She realized that there was also a moment in which they had to act or the need to act upon that feeling passed. An ember either caught fire or failed into oblivion. What if her father, as one example, had been interrupted during the introduction to her mother, or he had been swept away by friends before they could converse? Would he have swum against the current, against protocol, and returned to her side long enough to charm her? It is more likely that he would have reserved his flirtation for the next appealing introduction. Out of indecision or nervousness tonight, Ashton had waited too long. Expectation had grown so rapidly that it now stood between them, as large and unmovable as a boulder the size of a room. Yes, it was over. Ashton would eventually succumb to a woman bright enough, beautiful enough, and appropriate enough to satisfy both him and his mother. Jane would live the deteriorating life of a single woman of meager means.

"Do I understand from what we saw yesterday that you will be hauling cattle to the market by air?" Her words sparkled in the deepening twilight, revealing nothing of her disappointment but rather the lively curiosity that marked her normal queries.

"Trying to determine the feasibility of a hot-air balloon in moving every kind of cargo. That was my intent from the moment we saw it in Bath." She noticed the word *we* but dismissed it. She could not start that again. "As I suspected," he said, "the winds are too fickle for sustained use. Perhaps balloons have application in special circumstances. We could have used one on *Diamond Rock* to lift those impossible cannons." Another *we*. So he meant the word in an encompassing, not personal, way.

Jane began to shiver in her afternoon dress and light shawl. The breeze had picked up. The stone bench chilled her legs. The delectable cool had become a penetrating cold. It was time to walk down the hill, far more alone than when she had ventured up.

"It is settled," she said, rising. To his puzzlement, she added: "We have had our walk. We must return before it is too dark to see. It would not do for you to be like Jack. I would be held accountable if you returned safely from the war and then fell and broke your crown."

"J-Jane."

"Miss Austen."

"M-Miss Austen. If you please."

She turned to him.

"Will we not speak?"

"We have walked. We have sat. Outside of one or two pleasantries, you have said less than a lump of coal."

"But it is up to you."

"I have exhausted all of *my* pleasantries in an effort to *encourage* talk."

"Do you really want this to end?"

"An indefinable indefiniteness? Why would I not? I doubt either of us enjoys a life of ambiguity."

"Damn you, girl, release me!" She was certain his words would reverberate into the next county. "Release me and I will end the ambiguity soon enough!"

"Most certainly. You are released. Go where you will. Anywhere away from me!" She had not his thunder but she equaled his force.

He stumbled back. He pulled a packet of tattered letters from his jacket. "I showed these to Alethea. I wanted to be sure. She said you must finally love me. She said no honest woman would write as you had done. Unless you loved me." He raised his eyes, rich with tears. "You bade me come home, Jane. You must have meant to you."

"You are home, sir. Yet you do nothing about it."

Confusion draped his expression. He looked like a very large, very lost, child.

"Is it the new clergyman—Bridges? Must I put on the cloth to gain your attention?"

"There appears to be an ecclesiastical law that requires me to receive a clergyman's proposal on at least an annual basis. That does not mean I wish to have one—or accept it. I should despise Mr. Bridges regardless of any other considerations. Alethea should not have mentioned him to you. There is nothing to stand in the way of anything you may wish to say. Except for my frustration, now, that you have not wished to say anything."

"But there is! Do you not recall our last conversation?"

"I can recite your letters as if they were verse." The thought brought her as close to tears as he.

"The last time we spoke. Face to face." He pointed toward the big house. "In the library."

"It was terrible. We both said angry, stupid things. That was a different time. You were a brazen young man a little too impressed with himself. I was a disconcerted, *less young* woman a little too proud of herself. I forgave you long ago. I assumed you had forgiven me."

"You bid me never to bring up a certain subject ever again. You exacted a promise."

"Given all that has happened, it is madness to think I would hold you to that oath. Only obstinacy could justify your behavior tonight. Withholding the words that would bring us both joy—as punishment for my petulance long ago."

"I honor my word."

"I would sound a fool to say, 'Sir, you may now propose to me whenever you may wish. But surprise me, do.'"

"By your every word and deed you have insisted that I treat you as an equal. Equality and coyness cannot cohabitate."

"Ashton, I did not mean, I could not mean, half the things I said that day. I was spiteful to you out of guilt. You cannot possibly—"

"Except for your father, no one else has ever spoken to me with such clarity of meaning and exactitude of purpose."

One might suppose that his request for a formal withdrawal of her objection was necessary for his pride. After all, he had subjugated his pride in proposing to her originally; he had swallowed it entirely upon her withdrawal of the acceptance. His willingness to ask, yet again, represented the demolition of the entire edifice of Dennis family *honor,* for the many and considerable objections to the marriage remained intact. Yet as deeply as they had bitten, her heated words from the argument were not all from which he needed release, she sensed. His plaint went far deeper than a desire for her to take upon her own shoulders the dreadful things the people on her side had said and believed about him. *An unaccounted heart.* In all the world's dealings with this young man, she suddenly realized, no one had ever taken Ashton himself into account. His position, his wealth, his physical presence, his most demonstrative traits: yes. His humanity, his vulnerabilities, his feelings: no. Not even Jane had ever accounted for his heart. *Not even she.* Even now, *even now,* she had trouble seeing him not as a proposal, but as a person: a young man whose boisterousness was a shell that concealed his true, shy introversion.

"You would never acknowledge any of this to anyone but me, would you?" she said. "How much you have been hurt."

"My hurt is my private business."

She knew all too well her own humiliation resulting from their earlier involvement, yet she had not stopped to consider Ashton's. Her station in life had required her to take so much criticism that she presumed his wealth and standing would shield him from the same. From everything. Yet the public dismissal of criticism does not relieve the pain of that malice. Pain is not the exclusive province of the poor. When one appears to be made of granite, she thought, everyone must presume that one is granite through and through.

"You have served your penance, sweetest, dearest friend," she said. "You are released. You are free. To do whatever your heart desires. I want you to be happy. With me or anyone else. Do what brings you happiness."

Their exchange had taken them down the hill to the lake. The moon was high enough now to light their way. They embraced slowly, unreservedly. The emotion was more of relief than excitement. Their courtship had been more of a tiresome, muddy slog through winter storms than the carefree skipping of young love through the spring. But they had made it.

"K-k-kiss me, Jane. If you love me, k-k-kiss me."

She had never been kissed in any consequential way. Her father had offered hasty pecks upon her cheek; her mother had daubed her lips upon her forehead; Tom Lefroy—just the once, and so young and hurried and frightened were they that the kiss was like a brush against parchment. And of course Ashton had sought to kiss her in the library after their first engagement, oblivious to her effort to avoid him.

With her hands she drew his face down to her, noting the texture of his scar. His mouth was large; yet as he shaped his lips to hers, she felt a rush of warmth that brought her to shape her lips in return to his.

He had her sit on one of the many benches that were interspersed within the formal garden. She did not care about the cold anymore. Before her were flowers, nearly black by moonlight; behind her were a stone cherub and a topiary that swirled like the headdress of an Oriental queen. Bathed by a gibbous moon, Jane had her proposal and Ashton had his acceptance.

They held hands the last short way back to the house.

"You will not lie awake all night with your sister talking yourself out of this engagement?"

"No."

"You will not arrive at my office in the morning to renegotiate terms?"

"I will arrive to pester you with kisses."

"If you change your mind again, I will stuff you and Cassandra into a burlap bag and toss you into the lake like excess kittens. I will throw myself in after you. It will be the scandal to end all scandals."

"We are done with scandal."

"Then it *is* done?"

"I give my word, Mr. Dennis. Till death do us part."

Chapter 23

Every wedding with which Jane had ever been involved had been marked by a fluster of preparations, but the haste of her own wedding took confusion and female consternation to the highest degree. Though she and Ashton both desired the traditional, simple affair with only limited family and the closest of friends, the extent of the Austen clan and the voluminous number of commercial, scientific, and political acquaintances on the Dennis side culminated in a guest list the size of a bustling village. Not for the wedding itself, of course, which remained limited to family, but for the festivities that were to be carried on around the nuptials. For every two or three names removed by the couple as being too distant an acquaintance or relation, another dozen somehow became inscribed in their place. Mrs. Dennis, confronted with a fait accompli, determined that the wedding would be the biggest event in southeast England since the landing of William the Conqueror (who, if he were still extant, would have received an invitation too). Finally, the bride and groom capitulated. Their marriage was for themselves; the wedding, for Ashton's mother. This was, in Mrs. Dennis's eyes, the presentation of her son to society. In this context, the name and social status of the bride were inconsequential.

While Mrs. Dennis continued to issue invitations, and Alethea set herself to establish the military-like organization necessary to handle on short notice the burgeoning list of guests, Jane and Cassandra hurried to London where, with Eliza's help, they searched for her wedding dress. Initially, Jane wanted something simple—a replication of the red woolen dress that her mother had worn at her own wedding. Like most wedding dresses, her mother's had carried on in ordinary use for several years, then was relegated to a gardening dress, and finally was cut down into a riding outfit for Frank when he was a boy. This was the childhood recollection that provided the pleasant associations for Jane. Cass and Eliza quickly disabused her of the notion of a plain-spoken ensemble. "You cannot embarrass Ashton by wearing something fit for his maids," Eliza said. To which Cassandra added: "If you do not choose something gorgeous, then Mrs. Dennis—or your own Aunt Perrot—will choose something for you that will be ridiculously expensive and twenty years out of style."

It did not take any more than those brief admonitions to convince the bride-to-be. She knew full well that she had to dress in keeping with her new station rather than her old. But she was of the culture that required a woman to be encouraged to spend, rather than from the culture that presumed to spend. It was another sense of restraint she had inherited from her mother, who never accepted any invitation without at least one preliminary demurral. Cass and Eliza's excited encouragement was needed in order for Jane to submit to the full delight of visiting extravagant shops.

After a week in which they examined material for a number of lovely but not quite perfect dresses at Miss Hare's and Mrs. Tickars', they found what they sought at the most exclusive emporium in London, Véronique's. It was bright yellow material of a design originally made for royalty, a color that enriched her skin tones (which were unaccountably darker than the rest of her pale family) and made her hazel eyes shine. At the last moment, concerned that yellow would be more appropriate for a spring wedding, Jane nearly settled for a dark green gown that hearkened to the earthen tones of autumn. "You are going to wear the beautiful one," Eliza said. "For a beautiful bride. No more playing the coquette." The dress was yellow lamé on net atop a foundation of yellow silk. The body and sleeves were trimmed with needlepoint Brussels lace in a design of shells and flowers, the pattern of which was matched in gold lamé embroidery along the neckline, the sleeves, and the hem. The sleeves were shorter than the typical dress of the period, highlighting her long slim forearms and elegant fingers. The manteau was of fine yellow fabric lined with white satin; the embroidery on the border matched that on the dress. The shoes were gold. The finishing touch was a handmade veil featuring a repeating design of cornucopia and flowers—"be fruitful and multiply," Cassandra said. The veil was so lovely it refused to be left behind. It took a surfeit of pound notes to ensure that the dress would be constructed and delivered in time. Cass was delegated to keep watch over the progress.

Any trepidation that Jane might have felt at the expense or seeming ostentation in the choice of her gown—or any concern as to how she might have looked in comparison to a younger bride—evaporated weeks later when Ashton's eyes lit up as she came down the aisle. Very well, she thought. It sometimes happens that a woman is handsomer at nine and twenty than she was ten years before. That was the moment she remembered with clarity when, years later, the wedding and its subsidiary events had dimmed into a patchwork quilt of interesting but inconsequential proceedings. Ashton's eyes: They caused her heart to accelerate after a day of thoughtful calm. It was curious how little a bride had to do on the day of her nuptials except to be pampered, dressed, and given directions. Though she had never understood the brides who felt histrionics to be the *raison d'être* for the day, nevertheless she did not expect to be as detachedly amused at all the anxiety about her as she actually was. Cassandra, Alethea, and of course Mrs. Dennis acted as though any failure to achieve perfection with the lodgings, the food, the procession, the flowers, or the breakfast would result in a firing squad for *someone*, yet for Jane all that mattered was the exchange of vows. Everything else was a lovely addition, nothing more. Indeed, those vows represented the confidence she felt in the two of them as a couple. Those words would not unite them; they would confirm the unity that already existed. She believed their concord would present a joyous face to a welcoming society; but if for some reason they were to find themselves still alone against the world, there was no one she would rather stand up with than her husband-to-be. No one would ever split them asunder.

Together, forever. Those were the words in her head as Ashton's riveting gaze guided her the last few steps to his side. She had picked up glimpses of Henry and Eliza, Edward and Elizabeth and their large brood, Alethea and Ashton's other sisters, and Cassandra, all beaming. Their small band of true friends. Aunt and uncle Leigh-Perrot stood beside her mother, who was smiling wistfully, in muted gray that honored her father, gone not quite a year. On the other side stood Ashton's squat mother, dressed all in green and wearing a hat festooned with flowers, a toad hiding under the foliage. This image, as Jane swept by, enabled her to give Mrs. Dennis the most heartfelt of smiles.

The ceremony proceeded through the rolling cadences of the Anglican Book of Common Prayer. As a clergyman's daughter who often had helped fill a sparse church, and as an attendee of more weddings than she could recount, Jane could have recited the entire service from memory. Once or twice she almost jumped in to hurry along the officiant, her brother James. His raised eyebrow was all it took to settle her down. Ashton's recitation was slow but diligent, as weeks of practice forced the words into their proper shapes. He faltered only once, over *to love and to cherish*, not because he stuttered but because his voice broke. Jane said the vows in the musical tones of a professional, for she wanted him to hear her love in the perfection of her voice. She too, however, broke at the same words, *to love and to cherish*, bringing supportive laughter from James and the congregation. Soon enough, sooner than she could have imagined after more than a decade of anticipation as a single woman, she stood next to Ashton facing their families, wife to his husband.

Taking him in fully with her eyes one final time before they began their walk out of the church, she understood how desperate she was for him, and how desperately nervous she was about what exactly that might mean.

The hair was brushed, the maid sent away, and Jane prepared for bed. She told herself that the situation was essentially the same as the thousands of times that she and her sister had prepared for the night together. This mental digression was not intended to be convincing, merely to keep, for as long as possible, her mind off the reality that the situation *was* appreciably different. She neither looked nor made a point of *not* looking at the sight of Ashton disrobing on the opposite side of the room. She established his location primarily by sound: a boot protesting its removal, the whispering of a shed shirt, the fire's reaction to being stoked.

In their night clothes, wife and husband arrived at the bed simultaneously. Both hesitated, like two young children being newly introduced.

"Do you prefer a particular side?" Ashton finally asked.

"Whichever one you find less desirable."

"Neither side will be less *desirable* tonight."

"Ashton."

"A husband should defer to his wife's predilection."

"As a wife should to her husband's."

"My predilection is to please you."

"My predilection is to decide before we freeze to death."

Having noticed that she had started as if by habit toward the left, Ashton stepped around and entered from the right. The bed gave way against his weight. He held up the blankets for her to enter. She slipped in beside him. Despite the wood flaring in the fireplace, the sheets were appallingly cold. Ashton drew her to him and surrounded her with his limbs. His warmth was welcome and yet unsettling. Her affection for him was now so fixed and his touch was now so compelling that there was no question of her desire to become his wife in every way. She entertained no mystery or suspense as to what this meant literally, the immediate duties of a bride. Raised a farm girl, she carried no illusions as to the manner in which God enabled His creations to beget new generations. And in her wanderings through the countryside she had, in truth, been unable to immediately turn away when she once saw a yeoman bend a milkmaid over a low wall. ... Yet at the same time ...

The matter was different when it involved her own person, when it involved submitting—subjecting, allowing, encouraging?—herself to be handled in a way that was foreign to her experience and, for all she knew, averse to her inclinations. Torn between apprehension and an unexpected eagerness, between an obligation that came with the vows she took in earnest and a genuine desire to experience what was to come next, she expected, if nothing else, to carry on until matters were concluded with what she trusted was satisfaction for the man she loved. Was she a reluctant or foolish bride to face these moments with stoicism, or was she merely a nervous one? From the whispers of her married friends she had obtained the intimation that she might one day find the function of a mate to be less than disagreeable. In that lay her one best hope.

Resolute in her desire to prevent her husband from sensing anything less than her most earnest consideration, she asked, barely audibly: "Well?" She would never be remiss in her duty, though the precise steps to achieve that duty were unclear to her, even at this tender moment.

Ashton stroked her with a gentleness that was as surprising as it was provocative. To her dismay, her reaction did not correspond to the composure she expected to maintain with the unfolding of events. She had the contrary instincts to plunge blindly ahead while at the same time to rush blindly away. The contradiction gave her a moment's pause as to her dedication to undertake what she accepted as a matrimonial inevitability. Their marriage night was here. The vows they had taken were about to be completed. The naturalness of what should follow did not keep her pulse from accelerating. She found herself taking short, shallow breaths, as if she lacked the strength to fully respire. This *something* had remained in her mind from the instant she saw Ashton at the beginning of the wedding service. Despite her pleasure at that moment, despite the dizziness she had felt at the light that broke from his scarred face, despite the unsettling glow that had sparkled within her at his eyes' entrainment, she had not let the implication of their formal commitment sink in. Consummation had remained, through the wedding ceremony, a dream, a distant vista glimpsed through the haze of both fear and expectation: a vista that might be pleasing or might not, depending on so many things she had begun to feel and yet shied away from as an untried horse might shy at the prospect of a precipitous slope.

What she had sensed till now was the shadow of the thing, not the thing itself. Until this instant, *it* had not been something to be dealt with, to be confronted directly in the juxtaposition of male and female flesh. Not until now had she grappled with the immediacy of her fate, of the act that would change her life forever. Not until now, feeling him around her, his energy latent, did she fully comprehend that *he was a man.* He was a man, she was a woman, and this is why they were created. *Why did she not feel joy?* Rather, why did she feel so much fear along with the joy? Until now she had not doubted that she would want to be with him, or at least be happy to comply with his needs; but until now she had not been confronted with his awful physicality. Had this been a terrible mistake after all?

For an instant she thought to protest. She thought to reverse her acceptance of him still again, to flee once more to the safety of Bath. As she had once yearned for a husband, she now yearned for a return to the tranquil state of the innocent dance-floor flirt, of the charming garden conversationalist. Though his daunting stature implied otherwise, she had to believe that he would never compel her to undertake any action unsuitable to her ability or antagonistic to her humanity. If she wanted to leave, especially now, he would not wish her to stay. If she wanted to leave, like as not he would throw her out the door and slam it behind her. Yet he was a man. They were married. This was their wedding night. How could she anticipate that anything would happen except that which was going to happen?

"Are you all right?" Ashton whispered in a throaty voice.

"Yes," she said. "No."

After a few moments in which she could feel his warm breath on her neck, he said, "Y-you s-smell g-good."

"Attar of roses," she said. "From India. A gift, from my Aunt Perrot. Strangely enough, it was the favorite perfume of my other aunt, Eliza's mother. I remember the scent of it when I was a child. Hugging her was like launching oneself into a rosebush. Without the thorns, of course. I rather doubt that Aunt Perrot knows of this connection. Her usual attitude is to thwart genuine sentiment whenever possible."

Ashton nuzzled her neck. The effect was that of sheet lightning sending ripples of current through the rumbling clouds of her awareness.

"More important," she said, "is that it was specially ordered at great cost from a renowned *parfumerie*. Aunt Perrot is not in the habit of spending money on someone other than herself. It means she has finally forgiven me my many transgressions, which primarily entail my harboring the scent of the disreputable. How very odd that I speak of a metaphorical scent while describing an actual one."

"I cannot express my delight at discussing your ancient and parsimonious aunt," he said. "In bed. On our first night together."

"I do not mean to rattle on," Jane said, rattling on, "but she has been the source of much contention in my family. A good deal of which has revolved around one Mr. Ashton Dennis. I expect you to take what I am about to say the way in which I mean it, and not as if I speak in some vulgar manner. My marriage to a man of great wealth has redeemed me, and my family, in her eyes. We are finally worthy of being in the company of such a finely bred and aristocratic woman. I have achieved my life's ambition."

"I shall thank Aunt Perrot personally," Ashton said, with an inhalation so deep it might have drawn in her essence as well as her bouquet. "I shall sweep her into my arms and bless her for scenting my new bride so delightfully for our wedding night."

"You could never do such a thing!" Jane whispered fiercely. "She would faint dead away."

"Your Aunt is wiser than you think," Ashton said. "She gave you that fragrance for a reason. It wasn't to encourage the footman."

Jane could not risk more dialogue. For the first time in her life she was unable to play a conversation like a musical piece. She felt as a musician might feel if controlled by a puppeteer: flailing away, unable to stop banging out the notes. Something inside her was urging her on, though in what direction and for what purpose she could not say. After two or three deep breaths to compose herself—during which Ashton held himself with disciplined stillness, as if he understood that any abrupt move on his part might shatter her growing willingness to fully become his bride—Jane maneuvered herself to provide what she hoped was the easiest manner by which they could begin married life. Thus braced for his attentions, she closed her eyes and waited. ...

Until, after what seemed an eternity, there came a tap upon her shoulder.

"K-k-kiss me, Jane," he said. "Shouldn't we kiss? I would enjoy a kiss from my sweet, sweet girl. The first one we haven't had to steal."

She offered a quick kiss that would have been suitable for any family member.

"I've had better from my mother," he said. "And you know how little regard I feel for her."

Trying again, they achieved a kiss something like the one they had shared in the garden after their engagement. It was warm and personal, the way a man and woman kiss. But it could have been any man and any woman, in any garden. It caused them both, however, to launch toward each other simultaneously with such energy that they banged their teeth. They tried again. This time, as he pressed forward, she happened to withdraw. In consequence she became insistent as he became irresolute. By now Jane was eager to play the game, but neither one of them seemed to understand the rules. And then there was the matter of the hands. There were no places for Ashton to put his hands on her that did not embarrass, and she could not *imagine* what to do with hers. The two of them, Jane and Ashton, did not seem to be attempting romance so much as they seemed to be two uncomfortable actors pretending at romance in a poorly directed play.

She was puzzled. She had been expecting and to some extent dreading Ashton's ardency. His typical intensity should have taken them far down the garden path by now. Instead, they dawdled. The result was the same as if flowers were lacking nourishment: They were soon in danger of drooping. Ashton, she could tell, was keeping his distance—a small but noticeable distance. Why, she could not tell. Respect, perhaps, or delicacy. Almost as if he thought she might take the lead. As if she had any idea how. She indicated as best she could—lacking the words that normally served her well—that her enthusiasm was now more than sufficient for the undertaking at hand.

Abruptly, Ashton picked her up, blankets and all, and lifted her over to the fire.

"It seems you are always carrying me away from some disaster," she said sweetly, hoping that the reminder of their balloon adventure would induce the emotions necessary for the completion of what was developing into a trying enterprise.

"A disaster of my own making," he replied brusquely. He went to retrieve for each of them a glass of wine from the celebratory bottle (untouched on the table till now) that Eliza and Henry had given them earlier in the day.

"I have something I must tell you," he said.

Oh, dear, she thought.

Chapter 24

"It is my tendency to charge ahead toward my objective," Ashton said, as if they had been talking on a particular issue for some time.

"If you speak of tonight, your ambitions have been in no way … excessive."

"My overtures have been confusing and insufficient."

"But not unwelcome."

"Even if I am not sure of what I want, or how to obtain it, a vigorous initiative forces other people to stake out their positions," he said. "I speak of my behavior in general."

The emphasis of his speech must have been intended to convince her of a particular point, but she felt that the conversation involved someone else or a topic with which she was unfamiliar. To give herself a moment, she said: "I would not merit you with so calculated an action of your behavior in general. To provoke others into showing their hand."

"It was not intentional at first. I rushed ahead because I knew what I wanted and nothing else. But I could not help but notice the reaction. A forthright approach provides the only manner of achieving clarity in the world. … It is convenient to determine the mettle of the competition."

"When does a wife become a husband's competition?" she asked, her voice stirring.

"I am trying to work my way from the general to the particular. From my basic disposition in life to my behavior with you, tonight," he said with exasperation. "It is very unlike me not to take the initiative. Partly because—"

"—you defer to my predilections?—"

"—and partly because I do not know how." He stared into the wine as if seeking an answer in its blood-red eddies.

"It is unlikely that I am making it easy for you," Jane said, tiptoeing into a matter of great delicacy. "A naïve partner, even if willing, must inevitably engender frustration."

"I am a terrible dancer, despite years of practice, yet I thump across the floor with as much enthusiasm as a court dandy," Ashton said. He tossed his head as if to rid them of the distraction of her analogy. "I have no trouble acting on any subject about which I have knowledge," he continued, "and there are not many subjects with which I am unfamiliar. My hesitance does not stem from timidity. It stems from ignorance."

She did not quite catch his implication.

"Forgive them, Father, for they know not what they do. A wise prayer. I am trying to apologize, Jane, for precisely that fault. I know not what I do. If I am making matters difficult for you, it is not because I wish to. I genuinely wish to encourage an agreeable result. That is what I am trying to say. I have no knowledge of man and woman. The intimacies they are supposed to share. I know nothing of them. Of *it*."

"Of *it*—? Oh." She tried the wine to steady her nerves.

Now she understood the awkward and convoluted manner in which he was trying to contrast his formidable directness on most matters with his tentativeness toward her. He knows nothing of *it*? Surely, she thought with some bewilderment, it must have happened. His lonely days at Oxford; his regular travel to London, capital city of all that is lascivious; his overnight stops at inns with as many wenches to let as rooms; his passage through the tropic isles with cocoa-colored girls. "You are telling me that Mr. Ashton Dennis, the squire of all Hampshire, the lord of the mercantile class, the natural philosopher and traveler of the globe, has never—?"

"Too shy to beg," he said, investigating the depths of his wine. "Too proud to pay."

She was not certain what to make of his confession. It was understood, though certainly never discussed, that the man would bring a certain kind of proficiency to the marital bed. Indeed, her one thread of optimism for their first night together was that he would have enough experience for the both of them.

To her look, which she thought was meditative, he said: "You needn't gloat."

She took his hand. "It offers a great deal of satisfaction to a new wife that you profess openly what other men would try hardest to conceal."

He shrugged at the lack of consolation to them both in her observation.

What a charming turn of events, she thought. It had not been the astute judgment of an experienced man to give her a measure of space in their initial interactions. It had been the bashful nature of a male five years her junior, one no more experienced in the arts of love than she. The situation was both endearing and frightening. "Talk about the blind leading the blind," she said. "The blind, deaf, and double dumb." She downed most of her wine in one gulp.

He touched her in a manner that was familiar without being forward. "We are in this together, Mrs. Dennis," he said. She liked how that sounded, *Mrs. Dennis.* There were few words he could gentle so.

He continued. "We are both fully cognizant of the processes of the natural world. We both know how to execute, as it were, the mechanics of matrimony. That is not precisely the issue. I full well understand that you will not wish to go ahead as if the matter were another of my … contractual commitments. Contracts, and the world of men involved with them, are all I know. I do not like them much." He spoke in the brisk tones of someone delivering a lecture, yet there was tenderness in his touch upon her leg. There was something, too, in his eye that was fraught with emotion. "I am not so much of a dunce that I do not recognize the need for an *emotional* connection, a *spiritual* connection. … We drew close through our letters. They meant more to me than you can know. I understand that you may need more than words, now that we are here, face to face, as it were. As it is. You may well require a deeper … " He paused as if searching for more adjectives that might delay his conclusion. Unable to find any, he hurried on: "…a deeper connection that would make you wish to … c-cleave t-together w-with your h-husband."

He took a loud sup on his wine. "I want to assure you that my sentiments are in accord." He forced out his sentence with such alacrity that the words suffered almost no individuation: "I-do-not-wish-to-*take*-you-as-my-wife. I-wish-for-you-to-*give*-yourself-to-me." He took a deep breath as if exhausted by a difficult recitation. After the briefest of pauses, he spoke again, as if having momentarily forgotten the last line: "Whenever and however you choose."

His expression indicated a lack of certainty as to whether his sense was clear.

She remained silent, contemplative.

"Whenever and however you choose," he said with more conviction.

"An increase in volume does not improve comprehension," she said.

A frown creased his mouth. He began to arise, as if understanding that he should return to bed alone.

She stopped him and pointed to their glasses. "Do not be in such a hurry, Mr. Dennis. No woman has ever been wooed with such words, or so moved by their effect."

———~w·o-ᴄᴇᴛᴏ-ᴏ╳ᴇᴏ-o·ᴡᴡ———

Their wedding night became multiple (and absorbed as well the intervening afternoon), during which time they lay together as intimates, not quite but ever closer to becoming man and wife. At first the juxtaposition of elbows and knees, and the odd intrusion of the nose, made companionableness a trial. Marital relations seemed to be as much about what to avoid in the dark as it was about what to find. But after a while their limbs became acquainted. Man and woman shed their clothes, as if the cocoons of an earlier stage of life. In the forgiving glow of firelight they absorbed the shock of naked flesh; what might have seemed abominable became sublime. They were encouraged, too, by the steady progress in osculation. The secret, they discovered, was not exertion but restraint. Their efforts turned on the moment when Jane kissed him with so little pressure that it might have tantalized a butterfly. Until then they had retained a certain chasteness of distance, as if their bodies awaited formal invitations. That isolation of experience in the kiss, that fusion of twin sensitivities onto one small soft surface, concentrated their intention. Their mouths opened. As they dissolved in exploration, she could feel every nuance of her lover's kind and most sensitive lips. She slipped into a world that was unlike anything she had ever experienced: the moist surprise of supple and unexplored sensation; the alarming taste of a man; the vibrating synchronicity of a twinned human pulse. She withdrew as if from an appalling and unexpected collision; but it was only long enough for her to breathe, to wonder at what had happened, and to plunge into the experience once again. Their mouths came alive. They learned together the electrical language of tease and tongue—that wicked yet warranted flick of his or hers, she was not sure and did not care. The intensity of awareness from this smallest of physical contacts gave her a hint of a union deeper and more intense than any she could have imagined.

They discovered, too, the marvelous uses of their hands. Jane learned that the musicality of the fingers extended far beyond the keyboard; when allowed to extemporize she could transform the aural signature of emotion into the physical chords of love. Ashton proved as deft as a harpist in the undulating melodies he studied upon the strings of her nerves. She came to be jealous of herself: If he lingered too long in one place, another part of her demanded a caress. Intellectual stimulus and kindly affection were qualities of a goodly life together, she had always believed, but she now perceived through her awakened senses that these attributes were by no means all, or even most of, what a union of corporeal creatures could be. She had never conceived of herself as a physical being in the manner that Ashton was: imposingly real, unequivocally present in the flesh. The physical world was there, and she was in it. But it was as though she had always been floating above, or perhaps through it. She was her mind and the thoughts and emotions of her mind. She had never mastered the bodily translation from her mind into actual *being.* Till now.

Their bodies drew together as if they and not the minds that drove them knew exactly what to do. Despite the difference in size and shape, they entwined as naturally and as tightly as whorls of a honeysuckle. By now their fumbling was so familiar it brought comfort rather than unease. Awkwardness became its own kind of dance. Through the most ancient and urgent inter-being of two persons, she was pulled from the world of shades and shadows into the earthly plane of real existence. Where life was not observed from across the ballroom or critiqued from the safety of a sofa. Where life was not an idea but a fact. Where people laughed and loved, cursed and cried, lived and died. She glimpsed for an instant, with the plangent lucidity of a reflection in a stream, the beauty and horror of the world that awaited her. How could she fail to throw herself into that exquisite reality? How could she not *drown* there? They reached the threshold, where the sharp introduction to love cost her an indrawn panicked breath and more moments of distraction—as Ashton whispered "I'm sorry, I'm sorry" even while continuing in rhythm to his apology—but she was swept forward past the discomfortable surprise. The momentary jolt fell behind in the onrushing passage of fear and joy, which swirled around them in an escapade of emotion.

Her lips quivered—silly but true—here it was, happening to her. Her lips quivered, and the muscles of her abdomen rippled—mice scampering up and down her belly!—her limbs began to tremble, and the trembling turned into tremors. She clawed forward, fearful that she might fly apart before she reached the end. Yet she approached that instant with a tranquil confidence. Like a nun in an earthquake, she thought. Making metaphors as her old existence collapsed around her, the process by which the word became flesh. She shook as one might from a violent chill or the direst of ailments, yet the cataclysm culminated in a numbing sweetness, a mad churning that tumbled her senses down rapids of pleasure while bathing her nerves in chocolate and cream. ...

When awareness again floated upward to the surface, when ecstasy, *ex stasis*, returned to *stasis*, she thought of the quaintness of Ashton's request, that she be willing to give herself to him. This act had turned out not to be an agreeable submission to another's needs but a determined affirmation of her own. This was not to deny her gratitude to her husband—husband, that word!—whose instincts, to contain and bolster her during her moments of greatest necessity, had enabled her to seize the rapture she had instinctively sought and knew as it overcame her that she deserved in the full honor of life.

She had meant to call out his name in love and appreciation, but she had become incapable of speech. In all of her upheaval she had lost the use of language. Her thanks were extended now in the manner in which her fingers traced languid patterns on his chest, her own kind of poem. This is what word play ought to be, she thought. He continued to lie still, breathing as deeply as a well. His eyes shone in the firelight.

"You may have discerned by now my willingness to cleave," she said, blowing hair from her eyes and finally able to talk.

"I might have just noticed, yes."

"How does it feel to stand by with the fire brigade as the barn burns down?" she asked.

"Rather warm," he said.

"How did you stay with me for so long?"

"By desperately thinking of something else."

"Come, my love."

Her supple move provided Ashton with ascendancy, which during her distress had naturally devolved upon her. If Jane's energies could be described as a small engine spinning rapidly, Ashton's were that of a huge locomotive turning over slowly with massive torque. His way was neither as long nor as meandering as hers had been, and it rolled onward with gathering momentum until it slammed to a conclusion that left them both perspiring and spent and the mattress half off the bed.

Jane was not sure what happened then with time. They must have both drifted off. They awoke long enough to make adjustments for blissful rest. They sought a goodnight kiss but missed for lack of strength. Before sleep overtook her again, she watched the fireplace coals succumb to the dark. She tried to decide what had been the more profound and revelatory of her experience: what she had undergone, or her sharing with Ashton what he, *her mate*, had undergone.

It is never either, she decided. It is always both.

Her home life before marriage had been content; she never imagined that the love of a man could mean more to her than filial affections. This is what she had always told herself, at least from that moment when it appeared inevitable that nothing more would come into her life except filial affections. Yet now, at the very beginning of her marriage, she had already been proven wonderfully, deliciously wrong.

What next, she wondered. Dear, dear God, what would life throw her way next?

End Volume I

The Marriage of Miss Jane Austen

Volume the Second

The second novel in *The Marriage of Miss Jane Austen* series explores the marital life of Ashton and Jane as they learn about each other and engage with the world beyond the country village.

While delving into the psyche of a thoughtful and passionate woman experiencing the reality of married life in the early 1800s, the book also explores the subjects that surfaced in Volume I. The slave trade, in particular, creates conflict as the husband and wife must choose between important personal relationships and their growing awareness of what slavery on far-off islands actually means.

Through Ashton's business enterprises, their lives become more entwined with the technological advances that gave birth to the Industrial Revolution; they see the good and bad effects of "progress" on the ordinary family. Conflicts between science and religion increase, while conservative aristocrats seek to stymie the influence of the rising mercantile class. Meanwhile, the never-ending war with France grinds away on England, affecting their existence more every day.

As their relationship develops, they also face the critical concern of any family of wealth: Will an heir be born to preserve the Dennis family's entailed estate?

The Marriage of Jane Austen: Volume the Second will be available in 2016.

See www.austenmarriage.com for previews of the next volume, blogs on the many topics introduced in this book, and other matters of interest related to the Georgian-Regency era.

Acknowledgments

Many warm thanks to early readers who offered thoughtful and helpful comments on drafts of the manuscript: Marianne Allison, Lynn Fulks, Susannah Fullerton, Hilary Gilmore, Anne Goldner, Shelley Hanrahan, Wendy Alden Hemingway, Paula Johanson, Patti Knollman, Claire Lematta, Lorchid Macri, Deb Mathis, Bev Maul, Jerry McConnell, Megan McKenzie, Linda O'Neill, Susan Priddy, and Sarah Jo Smith; and who shared their thoughts and feelings on matters that contributed significantly to the content: Julie Allport, Jacquie Braly, Rebecca Chaulet, Carrine Greason, Mary Falkenstein, Wendy Alden Hemingway, Patti Knollman, Cristina Lamoureux, and Patsy Lewellyn.

Others supported *The Marriage of Miss Jane Austen* in various ways, particularly in the marketing and promotion of the book: Megan McKenzie and her team at McKenzie Worldwide; Reese Mercer, Luke McCready, and Jennifer Houston of Five Talent; Sam Handelman; and Patrick Lord.

Printed in the United States
By Bookmasters